THE SHADOW OVE

I remembered Atal's w
unable to turn away. I w
screams from the city ros
but stare into the darkne
came!

It came, rushing from out the bowels of the terrified town, bringing a black and stinking wind that bowled over its fleeing enemies as if they had no weight at all. And God help me, I *saw* it! Blind but all-seeing – without legs yet running like flood water – the poisonous mouths in the bubbling mass – the fly-the-light beyond the wall. The sight of the thing was mind-blasting.

And what it *did* to the pitiful Leng-creatures!

By the same author

BRIAN LUMLEY

The Clock
of Dreams

Grafton
An Imprint of HarperCollins*Publishers*

Grafton
An Imprint of HarperCollins*Publishers*
77–85 Fulham Palace Road,
Hammersmith, London W6 8JB

Published by Grafton 1992
9 8 7 6 5 4 3 2 1

First published by
Jove/HBJ 1978

A catalogue record for this book
is available from the British Library

ISBN 0 586 21465 8

Set in Times

Printed in Great Britain by
HarperCollinsManufacturing Glasgow

For Barzai
the Not-so-Wise,
who proved – however
involuntarily – that what
goes up need not
necessarily
come down
again.

Contents

Introduction

Myself, I've never been much of a dreamer, never traveled far past Ulthar; but I have watched caravans fording the Skai, and I have sat in the smokeroom of the Inn of a Thousand Sleeping Cats and listened to the tales of my betters. I suppose most dreamers have. It's true, though, that there seem to be fewer of us around these days. Time was when a man of the waking world could guarantee that if he boarded at an inn in the land of Earth's dreams, sure enough he would find a fellow dreamer or two from the world of waking mortals; and wouldn't the tales fly thick and fast then? Yes, they surely would.

You would hear magical names of men and places – names to set your pulses pounding and your imagination tingling – and thrill to the telling of tales of heroic and fantastic deeds. And someone would be bound to mention Kuranes or Randolph Carter . . . or Richard Upton Pickman. And while you might shudder at the hinted fate of the latter, certainly you would also gasp in awe at the adventures of the others. Ah, those were the dreams . . .

Still, I suppose I shouldn't complain too bitterly, for when I come to think of it I heard two of my favorite tales quite recently, and as coincidence would have it I heard them at the Inn of a Thousand Sleeping Cats . . . in Ulthar.

The first was a strange tale and complicated, a tale of all the worlds of space and time, of strange dimensions and planes of existence beyond the ken of most men. A tale of motes in the multiverse swirling beyond barriers neither spacial nor temporal, nor of any intermediate dimension recognized by mortal man except in the wildest theories of science and metaphysics. A tale of paths between the spheres, dim corridors leading to equally dim and conjectural lands of elder myth . . . And yet all of these seemingly inaccessible places were just around the corner to the time-clock.

Indeed 'time-clock,' as Titus Crow had long since recognized the fact, was a completely inadequate misnomer for that – machine? A plaything of the elder Gods come down the ages from lands beyond legend, from a time beyond time as men reckon it, the clock was a gateway on – on everything! It was a door to worlds of wonder, joy and beauty – but it was also a dark pothole entrance to caves of innermost, alien evil and shrieking, unnameable horror.

The first tale I heard was the story of how the clock came into Henri-Laurent de Marigny's hands in the first place, and it is a tale already told. But for the sake of the unacquainted I will briefly reiterate it before taking up the second of the two stories proper. Before even that, however, I had better tell what little is known of the time-clock itself.

Certainly the clock's history is strange and obscure enough to whet the mental appetite of any lover of mysteries or would-be sounder of unfathomable wonders (which you must be, else you would not be reading this). First, tracing the existence of the weird – conveyance? – back as far as possible in the light of incomplete knowledge, it seems to have belonged to one Yogi Hiamaldi, an Indian friend of the ill-fated Carolina mystic Harley Warren. Hiamaldi had been a member, along with Warren, of a psychic-phenomenist group in Boston about 1916–18; and he had sworn before all other members of that group that he alone of living men had been to Yian-Ho, crumbling remnant of eons long lost, and that he had borne away certain *things* from that grim and leering necropolis.

For reasons unknown, the Yogi had made a gift of the clock to one Etienne-Laurent de Marigny (perhaps the greatest ever American occultist and the father of one of the heroes of the story to follow), who kept it at the New Orleans retreat where his studies of the arcane sciences formed his primary purpose in life. How much he discovered of its secrets remains unknown, but after the elder de Marigny died the clock was sold, along with many another antique curiosity, to a French collector.

Here there is a gap in the history, for while many years later Titus Crow bought the clock at an auction of antique furniture in London, all of his subsequent attempts to discover the whereabouts of its previous Parisian owner were doomed to failure; it was as though the man had simply vanished off the face of the Earth.

Now then, of Titus Crow himself – a man with a positive genius for the discovery of dark lore, lost legends, and nighted myth-patterns, who will also feature prominently in my tale – much is known; but for now suffice it to mention that his protracted studies of the clock over many years of his life were such that the device became something of an obsession with him. Often in his earlier years Crow would sit in his study in the night, his chin in his hands as he gravely pondered the enigma of the peculiar, coffin-shaped, oddly-ticking monstrosity in the corner of the room; a 'clock,' of sorts, whose four hands moved in patterns patently divorced from any chronological system known or even guessed at by man, and his eyes would rove over the strange hieroglyphs that swept in intricate designs around the great clock's face.

When he was not at work on less baffling cases, always Titus Crow would return his attentions to the clock, and though usually such studies were in vain, they were not always complete failures. Often he believed himself on

11

the verge of a breakthrough – knowing that if he were right he would finally understand the alien intricacies governing his 'doorway on all space and time' – only to be frustrated in the final hour. And once he actually had the doubtful privilege of seeing the clock opened by two men of equally doubtful repute and intent, whose affairs in the world were fortunately soon terminated . . . but then at long last there came a genuine clue.

It was while he was working for the Wilmarth Foundation – a far-flung body of erudite men whose sole avowed intent and purpose was to rid the world, indeed the entire universe, of all remaining traces of an aeon-old evil, the surviving demonic forces and powers of the Cthulhu Cycle of Myth – that Titus Crow visited Miskatonic University in Arkham, Massachusetts. There, in one of the carefully guarded, great old occult volumes in the university's world-renowned library, he finally recognized a sequence of odd glyphs which at first he was startled, then delighted to note bore a striking resemblance to the figures on the dial of his huge clock. Moreover, the book bore translations of its own hieroglyphed passages in Latin!

Armed with this Rosetta-Stone knowledge, Crow had returned to London, where soon he was at work again disinterring many of the clock's centuries-buried mysteries. And he had been right, for that incredible device was indeed a vehicle: a space-time machine of sorts with principles more alien than the centers of stars, whose like we may at least conjecture upon.

Of his work on the clock at this time, he wrote to his friend and colleague, Henri-Laurent de Marigny: 'I am in the position of a Neanderthal studying the operational handbook of a passenger-carrying aircraft – except I have no handbook!' And Henri was unable to assist his learned friend, for while his father had once owned the selfsame clock, that had been when he was a boy, and he could remember nothing of it. Titus Crow, however, was never a man to be denied anything once he set his mind after it, and so he had persevered.

And little by little he discovered all of the clock's peculiar secrets. He learned how to open its frontal panel, without suffering any of the many possible consequences, allowing the strange lights which invariably illuminated its interior to flood out in eerie shades that dappled his study with alien hues. He knew how to attune himself 'telepathically' to the device's sub-ethereal vibrations: how to 'make himself one,' as he had it, with the clock. He was aware of the nature of the 'commands' he must give to the clock to guide it on its journeyings through temporal and spacial voids, so that the time soon came when he believed he might attempt his first flight in the weird vehicle.

All of this knowledge came to Titus Crow in the very nick of time, for no sooner was he psychically ready to test his theories than just such a test was forced upon him. It happened when he and his young friend de Marigny (also a member of the Wilmarth Foundation) were staying at Blowne House, Crow's sprawling bungalow home on Leonard's Heath in London.

The two of them had grown to be very painful thorns in the sides of the deities or demons of the Cthulhu Cycle, and at last the prime member of that cycle, dread Cthulhu himself, had discovered a way to strike back at them. Dreaming hideously in R'lyeh, his 'house' drowned somewhere in the vast Pacific, Cthulhu worked his evil plot through Ithaqua the Wind-Walker, Lord of the Snows. For while Ithaqua himself was unable to go abroad beyond barriers immemorially imposed by the Elder Gods – that is, while he was restricted in his movements to the Arctic Circle and its adjacent environs, and to strange Boreal starlanes and alien worlds – nonetheless he was still undisputed master of all the world's winds. And now he sent elementals of the air

13

from the four corners of the sky to attack Titus Crow's home.

Left with no choice but to risk the doubtful sanctuary of the time-clock – as eerie shapes of evil formed beyond the shattering windows, monstrous forces that pounded at the shuddering frame of his bungalow retreat until Blowne House fell about his ears – Crow stepped beyond the open front panel of his vehicle and bade de Marigny follow him. And when that 'freak localized storm' had expired and the house was discovered in ruins, perhaps not surprisingly no trace could be found of the two friends; neither of them, nor of the weird clock.

Well, to cut a long story short, Titus Crow made good his escape from those monstrous minion winds of Ithaqua into the far future, traveling almost to the End of Time itself before finally he mastered the clock's many intricacies to control its flight. But as for de Marigny, he was not the adept that his friend was. Barely was their craft 'out of port,' as it were, before de Marigny was 'washed overboard' into terrible temporal tides – to be fished from the Thames more dead than alive *ten years later!* Though the flight in the time-clock had seemed to last mere seconds, and while Crow's younger friend had aged not at all, nevertheless ten years had sped by; which caused de Marigny to wonder *just how far* his friend had finally traveled – and was he perhaps still traveling?

It was not long before he was to learn the answers to these and to other questions.

Upon recovering from his fantastic ordeal, de Marigny went back to his old London home, and there one night a short time later Titus Crow also returned to the world of men. Ah, but this was a much-changed Titus Crow, for he had undergone a transition. Younger, stronger, wiser (though de Marigny found the latter hardly credible), the new Crow had seen marvels beyond belief, had traced his own lineage back to the very Elder Gods themselves. And

14

now he had returned to Earth for one reason only: to offer Henri-Laurent de Marigny the opportunity to join him in Elysia, the home of the Great Gods of Eld. As an inducement, if such were needed, this is how Crow had told his friend of his adventures:

'. . . I've been trapped on the shores of a prehistoric ocean, Henri, living on my wits and by hunting great crabs and spearing strange fishes, dodging the dinosaurs which in turn hunted me. And a billion years before that I inhabited a great rugose cone of a body, a living organism which was in fact a member of the Great Race that settled on Earth in unthinkable abysses of the past. I've seen the cruel and world-spanning empire of Tsan-Chan, three thousand years in the future, and beyond that the great dark vaults that loom at the end of time. I've talked telepathically with the super-intelligent mollusks of soupy Venusian oceans, which will not support even the most primitive life for another half-billion years; and I've stood on the bleak shores of those same seas ten million years later when they were sterile, after a great plague had destroyed all life on the entire planet . . .

'Why, I've come close to seeing the very birth of the universe, and almost its death! – and all of these wonders and others exist still just beyond the thin mists of time and space. This clock of mine sails those mists more bravely and surely than any Viking's dragonship ever crossed the gray North Sea. And you ask me what I mean when I talk of another trip, one involving yourself?

'When I return to Elysia, Henri, to the home of the Elder Gods in Orion, there will be a place for you in my palace there. Indeed, you shall have a palace of your own. And why not? The Gods mated with the daughters of men in the old days, didn't they? And won't you only be reversing the process? I did, my friend, and now the universe is mine. It can be yours, too . . .'

Soon after that Titus Crow took his departure from

Earth yet again, but this time he used the time-clock more properly as a 'gateway,' passing through it but yet leaving it behind until de Marigny should make up his mind one way or the other. If he decided to brave the machine's dark unknown, the way would not be easy. De Marigny knew that. But visions previously undreamed of had opened in his mind, and wonders beckoned and enticed him more magnetically than ever the Sirens lured Ulysses.

For de Marigny was a lover of mysteries no less than you, the reader, and as such could he possibly refuse the proffered challenge? Could you?

Part One

1

The Call of Kthanid

De Marigny had first flown the time-clock two weeks earlier under Titus Crow's expert tutelage. Now Crow was gone – back to Elysia and the incredible girl-goddess he loved there, Tiania – and de Marigny had decided to follow him, alone.

Crow had done a marvelous job of instruction during the brief flights he had shared with his friend in the clock, and de Marigny was by no means lost in regard to controlling that fantastic machine. It was simply a matter of 'meshing oneself' with the thing, so that the clock became an extension of its passenger's body and mind, an extra limb or sixth sense . . . or both.

Thus, while half the world slept and darkness covered the land, Henri-Laurent de Marigny set out to prove himself worthy of a new and higher life in Elysia; and he did so in the only way open to him, by pitting himself and his vessel against all the currents of space and time. The world, all unawares, dwindled behind him as he cruised out into the void in his strangely hybrid craft, his almost 'human' machine, and a wild enthusiasm and exhilaration filled him as he piloted that vessel in the direction of Orion. Somewhere out there – somewhere in the distant void, behind invisible hyperdimensional barriers – he knew that faerie Elysia waited for him, and it seemed only reasonable to de Marigny that since Elysia lay 'adjacent' to Orion, that star should mark his starting point.

On one thing de Marigny had already and irreversibly made up his mind: though Titus Crow had told him that in the event of insurmountable difficulties he could always contact him through the clock, he would not do so unless his life itself were threatened. From what he knew of it there seemed to be only one way into Elysia for a creature not born to it, and that was the way of peril. Only those who deserve Elysia may ever enjoy her elder wonders, and de Marigny did not intend to be dependant upon Titus Crow for his – birthright?

His birthright, yes – Elysia *was* his birthright, Crow had hinted as much. What was it his friend had said to him? 'Lover of mysteries you are, Henri, as your father before you. And I'll tell you something, something which you really ought to have guessed before now. There's that in you that hearkens back into dim abysses of time, a spark whose fire burns still in Elysia. And one more thing you should know.

'Those places of fantasy and dream I've mentioned – they're all as real and solid in their way as the very ground beneath your feet. The Lands of Dream, after all, are only dimensions lying parallel to the Worlds of Reality. Ah, but there are dreamers and there are dreamers, my friend, and your father was a great dreamer. *He still is – for he is a Lord of Ilek-Vad, Counselor to his great friend Randolph Carter, who is himself a just and honored king!*

'I intend to visit them there one day, in Ilek-Vad deep in Earth's dreamland, and when I do you can be with me . . .'

Musing on these things that Crow had told him, physically and emotionally weary now that the initial stage of his flight was successfully completed and the journey safely underway, de Marigny lay back and watched with his mind's eye – which was now a part of the time-clock's equipment, a mental 'scanner' of sorts – as the stars visibly moved in the inky blackness about him, so tremendous was the velocity of his craft as it hurtled through the airless, frozen deeps.

'As real and solid as the very ground beneath your feet,' Crow had said of dreams. Well, if Titus Crow said it was so, then it was so. And hadn't Gerhard Schrach hinted much the same thing back in the thirties, and other great thinkers and philosophers before him? Certainly they had. De Marigny could remember Schrach's very words on the subject:

'. . . My own dreams being particularly vivid and real – to such an extent that I never know for sure whether or not I am dreaming until I wake up – I would not like to argue which world is the more vital: the waking world or the world of dream. Certainly the waking world appears to be the more solid – but consider what science tells us about the atomic make-up of so-called solids . . . and what are you left with?'

And with thoughts such as these swirling in his head, and the fascinating panoply of vasty voids sprinkled with a myriad jewels in his mind's eye, de Marigny bade the clock speed on and drifted into a sleep; a sleep which seemed eagerly to open its arms to him, and one which was far from dreamless.

Beyond the slightest shadow of a doubt the slumbering de Marigny's dreams were not natural ones, and but for his previous knowledge of Elysia, passed on to him through Titus Crow – particularly of the Hall of Crystal and Pearl, wherein Kthanid the Elder God Eminence had his seat in an inviolable sanctuary beneath a great glacier – certainly he must have considered himself the victim of vilest nightmare. For the thing upon which he suddenly found himself gazing was a shape of primal horror, the blasphemous shape of Cthulhu himself – except that it was not Cthulhu but Kthanid, and where the former was black as the pit the latter shone with the light of stars.

Thus, while his subconscious body hurtled through the star-voids within the spacetime-defying matrix of the great clock, de Marigny's dreaming mind was present in that very Hall of Crystal and Pearl which Titus Crow had described to him in so much detail. And he saw that Crow had painted an almost perfect picture of that magnificently alien palace beneath the ice of Elysia's 'polar' regions.

Here was the massive high-arched ceiling, the Titan-paved floor of great hexagonal flags, the ornate columns rising to support high balconies which glowed partially hidden in rose-quartz mists and pearly hazes. And everywhere were the white, pink, and blood hues of crystal, strangely diffused in all those weird angles and proportions that Crow had spoken of. Even the hall's centerpiece – the vast scarlet cushion with its huge, milky crystal ball – was just as Crow had described it. And of course, Kthanid was there, too . . .

Kthanid the Eminence, Elder God and cousin to Great Cthulhu – indeed of the same strain of cosmic spawn that bred the Lord of R'lyeh – moved massively in the Cyclopean hall. His body was mountainous! And yet his folded-back, fantastic wings trembled in seeming agitation as Kthanid paced the enormous flags, his great octopoid head, with its proliferation of face-tentacles, turning this way and that in what was plainly consternation.

But for all that this Being was alien beyond words, what might easily have been horrific was in fact magnificent! For this great creature, bejeweled and glittering as though dusted with diamonds, stared out upon the hall through huge eyes that glowed like molten gold; eyes filled with compassion and love – yes, and fear – almost impossible to imagine as existing within so terrible a fleshly house. And those eyes returned again and again to peer intently at the lustrous crystal upon its scarlet cushion.

It was because of Kthanid's eyes that de Marigny knew – was certain – that there was nothing to fear here, and he knew too that this was much more than merely a dream. It was as if he had been called into the Elder God's presence, and no sooner had this thought occurred to the dreamer than the Eminence turned and stared straight at him where his disembodied being 'stood' invisible within the vast subterranean vault.

'Henri-Laurent de Marigny,' a rumbling but infinitely kindly voice spoke in the dreamer's mind. 'Man of Earth, is it you? Yes, I see that it is. You have answered my summons, which is good, for that was a test I had intended to set you before – before –' The mental voice faded into uncertain silence.

'Kthanid,' de Marigny spoke up, unsure as to how to address the mythical Being, 'I see that you are . . . disturbed. Why have you called me here? Has the trouble to do with Titus Crow?'

'With Titus, yes, and with Tiania, whom I love as a father. But come,' the great voice took on urgency, 'look into the crystal and tell me what you see.'

Disembodied, nevertheless de Marigny found that he was capable of movement. He followed Kthanid to the edge of the great cushion, then moved on across its silken expanse to the center. There the huge, milky crystal ball reposed, its surface opaque and slowly mobile, as a reflection of dense clouds mirrored in a still lake.

'Look!' the Eminence commanded yet again, and slowly the milky clouds began to part, revealing . . .

The dreaming de Marigny gazed upon a scene that filled him with icy dread, a scene he could understand even less than he could believe it. The crystal on its scarlet cushion now burned with red fires of its own, and dark shadows danced as flames leaped high above four hugely flaring, blackly-forged flambeaux. These torches stood at the corners of a raised dais or altar, atop which a great reddish mass – a living, malignant jewel at least three feet across – pulsed evilly as it reflected the ruddy light of the torches. The thing seemed to be an impossibly vast ruby; and guarding it, patroling the round-cobbled square in which

23

the dais stood, were several squat, strangely-turbaned figures with awful wide-mouthed faces. At their belts these guardsmen wore viciously curving scimitars, and as they moved about the foot of the raised altar de Marigny saw that they paused occasionally to torment two ragged figures whose limbs were roped to irons hammered into the steps of the dais.

The horror and sick shock that de Marigny experienced had its source in these two figures; for one of them was certainly his great friend of olden adventures, Titus Crow, while the other – ruddily illuminated in the light of the flaring flambeaux, fantastically beautiful even in her present distress – must be the girl-goddess Tiania, late of Elysia. Then, as suddenly as it had come, while de Marigny tried desperately to commit all the vision's details to memory, the milky clouds rolled back across the crystal's surface and all was gone.

Away in the time-clock, still hurtling through the star-voids half a universe away in space and time, de Marigny's recumbent form sweated, tossed and turned; while in the great Hall of Crystal and Pearl his disembodied sub-conscious turned imploringly to Kthanid the Eminence to ask: 'But what does it mean? Where are they? And how did this –'

'*Hold!*' The great Being turned abruptly and for a moment his huge eyes were slits, glittering with something other than compassion or love. Kthanid was every inch a God, and de Marigny sensed that for a moment he had been very close to witnessing the release of awesome energies. The Elder God's frustration was a living force that the dreamer felt as surely as his waking body would feel the warmth of sunlight or the chill of a bitter wind. Then the golden eyes blinked rapidly and Kthanid's towering form trembled violently as he fought to bring his emotions under control.

'Hold, de Marigny,' the mental voice finally rumbled .

24

again, this time less forcefully, 'and I will explain all. But understand that every wasted moment increases their peril . . .'

Then the great voice seemed almost to become resigned, as if giving a telepathic shrug. 'Still, what other way is there? I must tell you as much as I know, for of course you are their one hope of salvation. Indeed, you will be the *instrument* of that salvation – if you are able. Have you the strength, de Marigny? Are you the man Titus Crow believes you to be? Would you really presume to enter Elysia? I tell you now, I am not unjust – but I love those two. Bring them back to me, and I will welcome you to Elysia as a son. Fail me, and –' again the mental shrug, 'and you remain a child of Earth all your days – *if* you live through your ordeal!'

'Whatever needs to be done to help Titus Crow – yes, and his Tiania – I'll try to do it,' the dreamer fervently answered. 'Wherever I need to go, I'll go there.'

'You will need to do more than merely try, de Marigny, and indeed there is far to go. When I have told you all I am able to tell, then you must be on your way – immediately.'

'And my destination?'

'Earth!'

'Earth?' the dreamer gaped. 'But –'

'Earth, yes, for your own homeworld is the only safe steppingstone to your ultimate destination, to the place where even now Titus Crow and Tiania face unknown terrors.' For a brief moment Kthanid paused, then he turned his golden eyes in the dreaming de Marigny's direction. 'Obviously your mind is receptive to telepathic attraction, man of Earth, else I could not have called you here to Elysia. But tell me, can you dream? Can you truly dream?'

'Can I dream? Why, I –'

'Your father was a great dreamer.'

'Titus Crow has told me much the same thing, but –'
de Marigny began, then paused as an astounding thought
came to him. 'Are you trying to tell me that Titus and
Tiania are –'

The great Being nodded: 'Yes, they are trapped in
Earth's dreamworld, de Marigny. To find them, free them,
and return them to Elysia unscathed, that is your quest.
One man against all Earth's dreamworld – which is also
the land of her nightmares!'

Dreams of Doom

'There is a way,' the Eminence continued, 'by means of which I can rapidly impress upon your mind all that I know of your . . . destination. It may be unpleasant in that you could be left with a headache, but other than that it is not dangerous. There is also a way to speed the process up immeasurably, and . . . But no, I fear your mind is not ready for that. It would probably destroy you.'

'Crow has told me how you – *revealed* – certain things to him,' de Marigny answered. 'Right here in this hall, I believe. I am ready for whatever it is you have to do to me.'

'Titus Crow's capacity was unbelievably high, even taking into account the fact that the strains of Eld ran strong in his blood. With him the process was very quick, almost instantaneous, but I would not dare to attempt such a process with you. That is not to belittle you, de Marigny: it is simply that if you are incapacitated, then nothing can save Titus Crow and Tiania. But in any case, your education will not take too long; my knowledge of Earth's dreamland is regrettably limited. The reason for this will soon become amply clear to you. Now come to me . . .'

As the dreamer drifted toward the alien Eminence, so that great Being's face-tentacles seemed to reach out to touch his disembodied mind. 'Steel yourself,' came Kthanid's warning in the instant before contact was made.

. . . *And immediately gates of strange knowledge opened in de Marigny's mind, through which streamed fantastic visions of nighted myth and legend, released from Kthanid's* mental storehouse of lore concerning Earth's dreamland. And though it was perfectly true that the Eminence knew comparatively little of that subconscious dimension, still it seemed to the disembodied Earthman that the Elder God must surely be omniscient in the ways of human dreams.

For as rapidly as his mind could accept it, de Marigny became heir to a wealth of information previously known only to certain seasoned travelers in dreamland, a dimension whose very fabric existed for and was sustained only by the minds of Earth's dreamers. He saw the continents, hills and mountains, rivers and oceans of dream, her fabulous countries, cities, and towns, and he saw the peoples who inhabited those ethereal regions. Amazingly, he even recognized some of the places he saw, remembering now adventures believed forgotten forever in olden dreams, just as the night is forgotten in the light of dawn's rays.

And so knowledge passed from the mind of the great Being into the mind of Henri-Laurent de Marigny. He was shown the Cavern of the Flame where, not far from the gates of the waking world, the bearded, pshent-bearing priests Nasht and Kaman-Thah offer up prayers and sacrifices to the capricious gods of dream that dwell in the clouds above Kadath. Yes, and an instant later, whirled away to the Cold Waste, he even glimpsed Kadath itself, forbidden to men, but was offered no guarantee of that hideous region's location. Not even Kthanid knew for certain in which area of spacetime Kadath lay.

Snatched away from Kadath in the space of a single heartbeat, de Marigny traversed the seven hundred steps to the Gates of Deeper Slumber; and beyond those steps the Enchanted Wood with its furtive Zoog inhabitants was made known to him. He was given to understand how the Zoogs – small and brown and indeterminate as they were – might be very important to his quest, for they were not unintelligent and their knowledge of Earth's dreamland

28

was prodigious. Moreover, the Zoogs were reputed to have access even to the waking world, knowing the two places where the dimensions of dream and reality merge; though mercifully, in consideration of their doubtful appetites, they could not journey far beyond the mysterious places of their own dimension.

Then the Enchanted Wood and its burrow-dwelling Zoogs were gone, and de Marigny was shown the resplendent city of Celephais in the valley of Ooth-Nargai beyond the Tanarian Hills. And he knew that Kuranes, himself once a legendary dreamer, reigned in Celephais, and that King Kuranes was renowned in all the lands of dream as the only man ever to transcend the star-gulfs and return sane. Gazing down upon Celephais from on high, de Marigny saw the glittering minarets of that splendid city and the galleys at anchor in the blue harbor, and Mount Aran where the ginkgos swayed in the breeze off the sea. And there was the singing, bubbling Naraxa with its tiny wooden bridges, wending its way to the sea; and there the city's bronze gates, beyond which onyx pavements wound away into a maze of curious streets and alleys.

But de Marigny was given precious little time to study Celephais, for no sooner had he glimpsed the city and its surroundings than he was whirled away, high over the Cerenarian Sea, whose billows rise up inexplicably to the heavens. There, among fleecy clouds tinted with rose, he was shown sky-floating Serannian, the pink marble city of the clouds, builded on that ethereal coast where the west wind flows into the sky; and he marveled at dream's wonders as he saw below, through breaks in roseate clouds, hills and rivers and cities of a rare beauty, dreaming gorgeously in brilliant sunshine.

And once again the scene quickly changed – so rapidly, indeed, that de Marigny was thrown in an instant from daylight into darkness – and now he knew that the land below him was none other than the icy desert plateau of

Leng, and he saw the horrible stone villages whose balefires flared up so evilly. Then, coming to him on an icy wind that seemed to freeze his very soul, he heard the rattling of strange bone instruments and the whine of cursed flutes, while a distant chanting of monstrous implications chilled him further yet.

For a moment, peering down in starkest horror, he thought he saw some inhuman thing writhing and blazing upon a stake in the heart of one of these balefires, while in the red shadows around monstrous figures jerked and cavorted to the hellish, wind-whipped music. De Marigny knew that the thing in the fire – whatever it was – screamed hideously as it roasted, and he was glad that the icy, howling wind kept those screams from him; and more glad when suddenly he was rushed away once more to other, less terrible visions.

Now he was relieved to behold the templed terraces of Zak, abode of forgotten dreams, where many of his own youthful dreams lingered still, gradually fading as all dreams must in the end. But before he could look too long or wistfully at Zak's dim visions, he felt himself borne irresistibly onward, to pass beneath twin headlands of crystal which rose up to meet high overhead in a resplendent arch; and then he found himself above the harbor of Sona-Nyl, blessed land of fancy. But since it could not have been deemed too important that he should look long upon Sona-Nyl, once again he was snatched away, without pause, on across the Southern Sea toward the Basalt Pillars of the West.

Now, some say that splendid Cathuria lies beyond the spot where those black columns tower from the ocean; but wiser dreamers are sure that the pillars are only a gateway, one which opens to a monstrous cataract where all dream's oceans fall abysmally away into awful voids outside the ordered universe. De Marigny knew these things at once, and he might have had the answer to the enigmatic problem

30

had he not found himself once more suddenly and without warning whirled away to the Enchanted Wood. Patently there was something else in that dark place that Kthanid would appraise him of, for now he found himself in an exceptionally unfrequented part of the wood, where even the Zoogs rarely ventured . . . and he was soon given to understand the reason for their caution.

Here the great squat oaks were very much thinned out, all of them dead or dying, and the whole area seemed covered wtih unnaturally luxuriant fungi, springing up from the dead ground and the mush of fallen, rotten trees. And there was a twilight and a silence here such as might have existed since time began; and in a sort of clearing a tremendous slab of stone lay on the forest's floor, bearing in its center a Titan iron ring all of three feet in diameter.

As de Marigny was shown the strange moss-obscured runes graven into the vast slab's surface, so the timeless quiet and oppressiveness of the place seemed to swell beyond endurance. He gazed upon those graven runes and, finally understanding, shuddered; for while one set of the glyphs was patently designed to keep something down beneath the slab, a second rune seemed to have the power to cancel out the first.

Then de Marigny's very soul shrank down within him, as if some monstrously alien symbol had been held out to it. And now he seemed to hear his own voice repeating a warning couplet from Abdul Alhazred's abhorrent *Necronomicon*: 'That is not dead which can eternal lie, and with strange aeons even death may die . . .' And he knew that there must be something singularly evil and damnable here, a connection between this hideous slab lost in an ensorcelled wood . . . and all the dread demons of the Cthulhu Cycle of Myth!

De Marigny was already more than well-acquainted with the CCD (the Cthulhu Cycle Deities, so designated by the Wilmarth Foundation) and now in an instant, faster

31

than Kthanid might have implanted such knowledge in his mind, there flashed through his memory the pantheon as he knew it:

First there was dread Cthulhu, prime member of the CCD, prisoned in drowned R'lyeh somewhere in the vast and unknown depths of Earth's inscrutable Pacific. Then there was Yogg-Sothoth, the 'all-in-one-and-one-in-all,' a creature hideous beyond imagining – so monstrous indeed that his true shape and aspect are forever hidden, behind a mask or congeries of iridescent globes – who inhabits a synthetic dimension created by the Elder Gods to be his eternal prison. Since Yogg-Sothoth's prison dimension lies parallel to both time and space, it is often obscurely hinted of him that he is coexistent with the entire span of the former medium and coterminous in all the latter.

Then, high and low in the ranks of the CCD and their minions, there were the following: Hastur the Unspeakable, an elemental of interstellar space and air, and allegedly half brother to Cthulhu; Dagon, an ancient aquatic survival worshipped once in his own right by the Philistines and the Phoenicians, now lord and master of the suboceanic Deep Ones in their various tasks, chiefly the guarding of R'lyeh's immemorially pressured tombs and sunken sepulchers; Cthylla, Cthulhu's 'secret seed,' his daughter; Shudde-M'ell, Nest-Master of the insidious Cthonian Burrowers Beneath; the Tind'losi Hounds; Hydra and Yibb-Tstll; Nyogtha and Tsathoggua; Lloigor, Zhar and Ithaqua; Glaaki, Daoloth, Thamuth-Djig, and many, many more.

The list was a long one and contained, along with these actual, physical representatives of Cthulhu's cycle, several purely symbolic figures endowed with equally awe-inspiring names and attributes of their own. Chiefly, these were Azathoth, Nyarlathotep, and Shub-Niggurath, which symbols the Wilmarth Foundation had explained away thus:

Azathoth, the 'supreme father' of the cycle and described

32

as a 'blind idiot god' – an 'amorphous blight of nethermost confusion blaspheming and bubbling at the center of all infinity' – was in fact the devastating power of the atom. It was nuclear fission, particularly the great atomic explosion that changed the perfect peace of the primal NOTHING *into a chaotic and continuously evolving universe: Azathoth – the Big Bang!*

Nyarlathotep – as his imperfectly anagrammatical name had early suggested to Titus Crow (albeit that this fact was entirely coincidental) was none other than the power of telepathy, and as such was known as the 'Great Messenger' of the CCD. Even after the rampaging members of the Cthulhu Cycle were put down and 'imprisoned' or 'banished' by the Elder Gods, Nyarlathotep had been left free to carry the messages of the CCD one to the other between their various prisons. How may one imprison purely mental power, telepathic thought?

Shub-Niggurath – known in the pantheon as a god of fertility, the 'black goat of the woods with a thousand young' – was in fact the power of miscegenation inherent in all the CCD since time immemorial. For in the old days did not the gods come down to mate with the daughters of men?

So, de Marigny saw again in his mind's eye all of these things and knew the truth of them, these and many other facts concerning the CCD. And he knew, too, why Titus Crow had braved the trans- or hyper-dimensional voids between Elysia's and Earth's dreamworlds – a voyage undertaken in the past only by two great seekers after knowledge and one fool, of which trio only one returned sane – for Crow's errand had been of the utmost importance. It had been to put an end to Cthulhu's incursions into the dreams of men. For since men first walked the Earth as true men they had dreamed and peopled the parallel dimension of dream with their own imaginings; and Cthulhu, seizing early upon his opportunity as he lay in dark slumbers of his own in sunken, blasphemous

R'lyeh, had achieved a certain mastery over dreams long before man mastered the mammoth.

But from the start Earth's dreamland had proven alien to Lord Cthulhu and had resisted him; for his were dreams of outer voids beyond the comprehension of men, and as such could invade human dreams only briefly. Also, many of dreamland's inhabitants – not the human dreamers themselves but the living figments of their dreams – were friendly toward men of the waking world and abhorred those concepts Cthulhu would introduce into their strange dimension of myth and fancy.

So the Lord of R'lyeh cloaked his schemes concerning Earth's dreamland in mysteries and obscurities, patiently going about his aeon-devised plan in so devious a fashion as to wear away the barriers of men's dreams, even as great oceans wear away continents. In this way he gradually introduced many utterly inhuman concepts into the dreamland, nightmares with which to intimidate the subconscious minds of certain men in the waking world. Thus, while Cthulhu himself could enter the dreamlands briefly, the evil concepts of his minion dreams would fester there forever; his, and those of his likewise 'imprisoned' cousins of the same dreadful cycle.

All of these things concerning Cthulhu and the CCD flashed through Henri-Laurent de Marigny's mind in a split second, but in the next instant he was snatched away yet again to visions just as strange if not so fearsome. And yet these, too, were fearsome enough.

He saw Ngranek's peak, and the great face carven in the mountain's gaunt side. He saw the hideously thin and noisome outlines of horned bat-shapes with barbed tails, flapping not altogether vaguely about the mountain, and he knew that these were the night-gaunts that guard Ngranek's secret. Then, as some of them flew closer, he saw that which made him shudder horribly: they had no faces!

But the bat-shapes did not acknowledge his presence,

and before they could draw too close he was rushed away again over the Peaks of Throk, whose needle pinnacles are the subject of many of dream's most awful fables. For these peaks, higher than any man might ever guess or believe, are known to guard the terrible valleys of the Dholes, whose shapes and outlines are often suspected but never seen. Then he soared down, down, and down, until his ears were filled with a vast rustling of Dholes amidst piles of dried-out bones . . . He knew then that this place he had swooped down to was none other than the Vale of Pnoth, into which ossuary all the ghouls of the waking world throw the remains of their nighted feastings; and he trembled violently as the rustling ceased momentarily – almost expectantly – just as the chirruping of crickets ceases at the tread of human feet.

But now the things de Marigny was experiencing were hastening one after the other through his mind at a dizzy pace, blurring as they went down upon his memory in fragmentary, erratic fashion. He was snatched up and out of the Dhole-infested Vale of Pnoth and away across dreamland in a frantic rush. In rapid procession he saw the oaken wharves of Hlanith, whose sailors are more like unto men of the waking world than any others in dreamland – and ruined, fearsome Sarkomand, whose broken basalt quays and crumbling sphinxes are remnant of a time long before the years of man – and the mountain Hatheg-Kla, whose peak Barzai the Wise once climbed, never to come down again. He saw Nir and Istharta, and the charnel Gardens of Zura where pleasure is unattainable. He saw Oriab in the Southern Sea, and infamous Thalarion of a thousand demon-cursed wonders, where the eidolon Lathi reigns. He saw all of these places and things and many more . . . and then there came a terrific, sickening whirling of his soul – following which de Marigny found himself dizzy and utterly disoriented back in the throneroom of Kthanid the Eminence in Elysia.

3

Journey Into Dream

'But why?' de Marigny asked the great Being. 'Why did Crow go into Earth's dreamland, and how? And what possessed him to take Tiania with him? And where *exactly* are they? I need to know these things if I'm to –'

'Hold, man of Earth,' Kthanid cut him off. 'As to your first question: I had thought to make that amply clear in what I have shown you, but obviously I failed. Crow went into Earth's dreamland to put an end to Cthulhu's insidious fouling of the dreams of men. He went where it was his birthright to go, just as it was his birthright to enter into Elysia. He went because the Lords of Elysia – which you know as Elder Gods, of which I am one – cannot go there themselves. We would be just as alien in your dreamland as is Cthulhu, and for that reason we will not enter it. If ever the time arrives when we *must* enter it, then the visit will be as brief as possible – as brief and unobtrusive as we can make it. There are reasons other than those I have mentioned, and one of them is this: the gateway between Elysia and the world of Earth's dreams has two sides. If we entered from Elysia, who can say what might or might not follow us back through the gate when we returned?

'As to why Titus Crow took Tiania with him, she would not let him go without her! And it will be to my eternal sorrow if aught of evil befall them, for it was I laid them to sleep here, and I assisted their dreaming minds across nightmare voids to your Earth and its dreamland.' As he spoke, Kthanid moved across the great hall to a small and curtained alcove. He drew aside the drapes to show de Marigny the forms of a man and woman where they lay in crystal containers, their heads resting upon silken cushions.

As his spirit eagerly drifted forward, it was as much of a 'physical' shock as it could be to the disembodied de Marigny to gaze upon the recumbent form of the man with whom he had shared so many strange adventures . . . and upon that of Titus Crow's woman, the girl-goddess Tiania. Despite the fact that he knew what he had seen of them in Kthanid's crystal was only a dream manifestation of the two, nevertheless it was an eerie experience to see their living, breathing bodies here in the Hall of Crystal and Pearl. Recovering himself, he moved closer.

Crow's handsome, leonine face and his form were well enough known to de Marigny, but Tiania was very new to him, a stranger. He looked upon her, awed. Kthanid felt the awe of de Marigny and understood the emotions the Earthman must feel. He knew that no mortal man could look upon Tiania and not be moved. And he was right. Tiania's figure and face were indescribably beautiful. Her eyes were closed now in dreams that brought troubled lines to her pale-pearl brow, but de Marigny was almost glad that she slept this uneasy sleep. He felt sure that to gaze into her eyes would be to drown quite helplessly. He knew that he could never forget her, that he would know her wherever and whenever he saw her again.

Her hair was a lustrous emerald ocean, cascading down the spun golden strand of her cape, and her mouth was a perfect Cupid's bow of pearl-dusted rose, lips parted slightly to show the whitest teeth de Marigny had ever seen. The girl's face formed a slender oval in which arcing emerald eyebrows melted into the verdure of her temples. She had elfin ears like petals of rare blooms, and a nose so delicate as to go almost unnoticed. She radiated a distillation of the very Essence of Woman, human and yet quite definitely alien. She *was* a woman, yes, and

37

not a goddess – but certainly the stuff of the Gods was in her. And she was the same woman he had glimpsed in Kthanid's crystal, helplessly staked out on the steps of the ruby altar in the distant world of Earth's dreamland. And just as she lay here now in this strange casket, so she had lain on those basalt steps – side by side with Titus Crow.

De Marigny turned suddenly to Kthanid to implore: 'But why don't you just wake them up? Surely that would get them out of there?'

Seeming quite human now, or as human as he could in his alien form, the great Being shook his head. 'No, de Marigny, it cannot be done. I have at my command every physical and psychical means by which such a recovery could be attempted, but they cannot be awakened. Do you think I have not tried? Something has them trapped there in Earth's dreamland, a force which defies every attempt I make to recall them. Here their subconscious bodies lie, rapt in evil dreams from which I am powerless to rouse them. The problems are many, de Marigny, and they are rare. First there is this unknown force that binds them to Earth's dreamland. Then there is the fact that they are separated from Elysia by vast alien voids of dream and all the horrors such voids harbor, and finally –'

'Yes?'

'We do not know their exact location. The same force that binds them to dream prevents detailed observation. I cannot name the region in which they are trapped. And Earth's dreamland is vast, de Marigny, wide-ranging as all the dreams of men have made it.'

'Then where do I begin?' de Marigny asked, perplexed. 'When? How?'

'Do not be too eager, Earthman. And, yes, perhaps I myself am too fearful for the safety of Tiania and your friend. What you saw in the crystal was a possible future, a possible occurrence yet to come. It has not gone so far, but in all the worlds of probability it will. I have searched the possible futures of Earth's dreamland as far as I dare, but only that one future ever presents itself for my viewing, and that one future draws ever closer. It is most certainly the same force that binds Titus and Tiania in dream that threatens their very existence.'

'Their very existence? But how can any real physical harm come to them when their bodies are here? I don't understand.'

Again (sadly, de Marigny thought) Kthanid shook his head. 'You seem to understand very little, Earthman.'

'You have to remember, Kthanid, that I'm not a great dreamer.'

'No, you are not,' the Eminence answered, again sadly. Then the great Being's thoughts brightened. 'But your father was; indeed he still is. And I believe that one day you will be, too.'

'That's all very well – and I thank you for your faith in me – but with all due respect, it doesn't help us much right now, does it? Look, you keep mentioning my father. I don't remember a great deal of him, but if it's true that he lives on in Earth's dreamland, well, surely he would be able to help me.'

'Etienne-Laurent de Marigny? Oh, yes, doubtless he would help you. Indeed, I am certain he would find a way to go to the aid of your friends – if he were able.'

De Marigny waited for Kthanid to continue, then shook his head at the great Being's silence. 'I still don't understand. My father is a lord in dreamland, surely. Trusted counselor to Randolph Carter, and –'

'Yes, that is so,' Kthanid interrupted, 'but there is a problem.'

'A problem?'

Kthanid offered what de Marigny took to be a nod, then continued. 'Ilek-Vad, where Randolph Carter wisely rules – and not only Ilek-Vad but Celephais and Dylath-Leen too – they are beyond my power to scan. This was not always so. Until quite recently, an Earthyear or so at most, I could look upon Ilek-Vad and Celephais in my crystal, but no longer. Dylath-Leen is different. For many years there has been some sort of screen about Dylath-Leen. Of two of these forcefields – I suppose that is what they must be – those about Ilek-Vad and Celephais, I know only this: that nothing gets either in or out. I do not wish to alarm you, young man, but for all I know of those places their inhabitants are no more, they may well have been stricken from the dreams of men. As for the third city, Dylath-Leen, I believe that the same force which obstructs me in attempting to locate Titus Crow and Tiania is also responsible for my inability clearly to scan Dylath-Leen. Yes, perhaps there is a connection there, de Marigny. Perhaps –'

'Perhaps that's where they are, in Dylath-Leen.'

'It would seem possible. You must look into it as soon as you can. Meanwhile, listen well to what I have to say. Remember that there are levels of dreaming, de Marigny, and that our lost friends must be in the very deeps of dream. A man might waken easily from the shallower levels, and he may be awakened even as he sinks into the abysses. But Titus and Tiania have penetrated to a region from which – for some reason as yet unknown, perhaps that *force* I have mentioned – they cannot escape unaided.

'In effect, this means that right now Earth's dreamland is more real to them than the waking world. Wherever they are you must find them; you must rendezvous with them there in the possible future that you saw in my crystal. It will not be easy.'

'Then let's waste no more time. Tell me how to go about it.'

'Yes, yes, in a moment. But before that there are certain things you must commit to memory. Firstly: in

40

Ulthar there is a very ancient man named Atal. Seek him out and ask him what you will. He is wise almost beyond wisdom and good beyond goodness. Secondly: beware of manifestations of Cthulhu or his devil's brood that you may come across, and remember that in the dreamlands even purely symbolic concepts may take form. Be particularly wary of Nyarlathotep! Thirdly: remember that you have Crow's flying cloak, and you have the time-clock, too. These should prove to be great weapons against any terrors dream may confront you with. As for the clock: why, Titus Crow can use that device in ways that confound even me! Finally: never forget that while many things are far simpler in dream, others are maddeningly difficult, almost impossible. Now, do you think you can remember these things?'

'Yes, and everything else you've showed me.'

'Good. As to how you may reach Earth's dreamland: first you must return to the time-clock, which you will then pilot back to Earth. I will of course assist you in your return to the time-clock, but from then on you will be on your own. I suggest you go into orbit about the planet Earth, after which . . . you will simply go to sleep. But as you drift into sleep you will command the clock to carry you *in the direction of dreamland!* Then you will sleep – and you will dream, de Marigny, you will dream.'

The Eminence paused, and after a moment de Marigny asked: 'And is that all?'

'That is all. Anything else would be a waste of time, superfluous, possibly dangerous. I do not know enough of your dreamland to say more. Now you must go back to the clock. Your quest begins, de Marigny. I wish you luck.'

Suddenly the great Being's face-tentacles spread outward from his face like the rays of a bright sun, and the lights of stars blazed in his eyes. De Marigny – or rather his Ka, or whatever it was of him that Kthanid had called to his glacier palace in Elysia's frozen regions

– was instantly dazzled. When finally he could see again, the scene before him was rapidly shrinking, dwindling down to nothing, so that soon even Kthanid was only a tiny, alien, jeweled creature that finally shrank away and vanished. Then there was nothing but a rushing darkness that seemed to last forever; and yet he knew when the rushing stopped and he found himself once more within the matrix of the time-clock that his journey had taken less than a second. Indeed, it had been instantaneous.

Without wasting a single moment, he turned the clock about and raced back through the voids of space toward the world of his origin. His heart began to beat wildly and his head started singing with exhilaration as he thought of the quest before him, and the reward at quest's end – to enter Elysia! Not once did he contemplate failure . . .

Some time later, in the Hall of Crystal and Pearl, Kthanid stood where de Marigny had last seen him. Now, however, no bright fires lit his golden eyes, and the lighting of the vast chamber itself was greatly subdued. Within the Eminence an unseen battle raged, and he trembled violently as he sought to calm himself. Of course he had done the right thing . . . or had he? After all, he owed no loyalty to the Earthman de Marigny . . . but then, neither was the man an enemy. Nor was his willingness to be faulted. Yet, if the problem was looked at in the right perspective it was immediately apparent that in the great scheme of things Henri-Laurent de Marigny was utterly insignificant. On the other hand . . .

For what must have been the fifth or sixth time since he had sent the disembodied de Marigny back to his Earthly body in the time-clock, Kthanid went to the huge cushion with its milky crystal and peered into translucent depths that quickly cleared to his gaze. And as before he drew back from the scene which repeated itself within the crystal's all-scanning eye. It was that same cruel scene de Marigny had gazed upon earlier, at least in all the details of its background. But whereas before two figures had lain stretched out on the basalt steps of the ruby dais, now there was only one. Kthanid could see the man's face quite clearly, and once more he trembled mightily as the battle within him welled up again. The fear-filled yet grimly determined face in the crystal was that of Kthanid's most recent visitor – Henri-Laurent de Marigny!

Finally, something gave within the great Being's heart; a decision like none he had ever made before was made. He uttered a word which only the Elder Gods themselves might ever repeat or understand, then snatched his eyes from the scene in the crystal. And in the next instant his golden eyes blazed brighter as, tapping the tremendous sources of his body's alien energies, he sent his mind racing out on a Great Thought across strange transdimensional gulfs and light-years of space.

Straight to the time-clock where it raced in orbit around the Earth Kthanid's mind sped – but too late. De Marigny was already fast asleep in the warm womb of his weird vessel. And while that vessel registered his body's presence, Kthanid knew that the real de Marigny was somewhere else, inhabitant now of Earth's mysterious dreamland. It was as it should be, as Kthanid had planned it to be, and yet . . . What use to call him back from dream now?

Feeling within himself a treachery as alien to his emotions as they were to those of the Earthman he felt he had betrayed, the Elder God rushed in a fury back to Elysia. There he closed his palace and his mind to all would-be visitations and sat alone in the vast Hall of Crystal and Pearl.

4

The Quest Begins

Night merged slowly into dawn in dreamland. To the east the very faintest of flushes tinted the sky gray, which was as well, for otherwise the night, except where it was studded with the bright jewels of fireflies, was of the very blackest.

At first de Marigny was disoriented, dazed; a lassitude was upon him. It was pleasant to do nothing but stand and admire the night and the first stirrings of a distant dawn. Then, as he drifted deeper into dream, he felt the night's chill and shivered at the luminous mist that began to swirl up eerily about his ankles. Then, he remembered his mission, and realized his supreme mistake. He was . . . alone! True, he still had Titus Crow's flying cloak about his shoulders, but where was the time-clock?

Suddenly complete realization of his plight filled him. He was lost in a nighted mist in some unknown region of Earth's vast dreamland, with only the fireflies for company and a ground mist that lapped at his ankles. And somehow he had lost his greatest hope of ever completing his mission; somehow he had left the fabulous time-clock behind him in the waking world.

How had it happened?

What was it Kthanid had said he must do? Yes, the Eminence had said: 'Command the clock to convey you in the direction of dreamland.' Well, he had done just as Kthanid had directed . . . hadn't he? Then, remembering, de Marigny groaned and cursed himself for a fool. The instructions he had given the clock had been wrong. He had simply ordered it to *transport* him to dreamland. And it had done just that. Without really knowing what he was doing, de Marigny had discovered Crow's method of using the clock more truly as a 'gateway.' For right now that alien vehicle was still in orbit around the Earth where he had left it, and de Marigny was stranded in dream just as surely as the friends he had come to rescue.

Perhaps if he had kept his head – if he had given the problem a little more studied thought – he might have seen a solution. For he was not yet too deeply drowned in dream to strike out for the surface, to waken himself up. Things are rarely perfectly clear in dream, however, and de Marigny was not an expert dreamer . . .

As the sky gradually lightened and the fireflies blinked out one by one, the adventurer found himself at the top of a great flight of steps that went down into a sea of mist. De Marigny knew those steps from older dreams forgotten until now, and more recently from his telepathic session with Kthanid. They were the seven hundred steps to the Gate of Deeper Slumber, beyond which lay the Enchanted Wood and those regions of dream which he sought.

De Marigny gritted his teeth and pulled Crow's cloak more warmly about his shoulders. Somewhere down there, beyond that wood at the foot of the steps, somewhere in those dreamlands spawned of the fantasies of a million dreamers, Titus Crow and Tiania of Elysia were or would soon be in desperate need of help, in peril of their very lives. There was only one course of action open to him.

Cautiously de Marigny descended the seven hundred steps and passed through the Gate of Deeper Slumber, and as the mist began to disperse and dawn grew more strongly beyond the trees, he set out through the groves of great gnarled oaks toward the far side of the Enchanted Wood, where he knew that the Skai rushed down from Lerion's slopes to Nir and Ulthar on the plain. Often as he pushed on through the wood, de Marigny heard the sounds that Zoogs make, but he saw not a one and was glad for that.

Often, too, he stumbled upon places where the trees were fallen into decay, and the ground was soggy with its burden of rotten oaks and alive with phosphorescent fungi. He would skirt these diseased areas, knowing that in one of them a massive slab of stone set with an iron ring of fantastic girth stood sentinel over nameless Cthonian things of hideous connections.

The wood was a fearsome place indeed, but while de Marigny was tempted again and again to use his flying cloak to climb above its suspected but unseen terrors, he refrained from doing so. He could not say what eyes might be watching him; he did not wish it known that a dreamer with a strange and wonderful flying cloak had entered dreamland. In any case, the sun was up now and the fears of the dark wood were disappearing along with the last wisps of mist.

It was a bright morning when he finally, wearily came out of the wood and set off across the rolling plains for Ulthar. He skirted Nir late in the morning, and as the sun approached its zenith crossed the Skai by means of an ancient wooden bridge. Hungry now, he was tempted to stop and rest at one of the many farms that dotted the plain; he had little doubt but that the friendly folk of these parts would find a meal for him. He did not stop, however, for the urgency of his mission was driving him relentlessly onward. And he did not know how long he had to effect the rescue of Titus Crow and the girl-goddess Tiania.

And so de Marigny came to Ulthar, the City of Cats, where an ancient ordinance has it that no man may kill a cat. It was quite obvious to the dreamer that this was indeed Ulthar, for even the outskirts were crowded with felines of every variety. Sleek females sunned themselves atop sloping roofs; young, careful-eyed toms kept cool while guarding their territories in shaded doorways; kittens tumbled comically in the long grass of the ornate gardens of rich personages. He paused very briefly in the suburbs to watch some of the kittens at their play; but then, having questioned a shopkeeper as to the whereabouts of the Temple of the Elder Ones, he hurried on into the city proper.

The Temple of the Elder Ones stood round and towering, of ivied stone, atop Ulthar's highest hill; and there, just within the temple's vast outer door, de Marigny was politely questioned by three young priests as to his purpose at the temple. He answered that he was from the waking world, that he sought audience with Atal the Ancient on very important matters. And when, in answer to further questioning, he told them his name the young priests grew wide-eyed indeed. One of them went hurriedly off into the dim and mysterious heart of the temple to seek an audience for de Marigny with the ailing high priest.

Finally the dreamer was taken to an inner sanctum where in a bed of finest silks lay the frail and weary shell of dreamland's wisest and oldest inhabitant. Now the younger priests departed, bowing themselves from the presence of their master and his visitor. Atal very gently propped himself up on his pillows to beckon de Marigny closer. When he could see the man from the waking world more clearly, he smiled feebly to himself, nodding in silent acknowledgment.

Eventually the ancient spoke, and his voice was like the rustle of late autumn leaves. 'Yes, yes – you are truly the son of your father.'

'You knew . . . you *know* my father?'

'Aye. Etienne-Laurent de Marigny, Lord of Ilek-Vad and Advisor in Chief to the king, Randolph Carter. He *is* your father, is he not?'

De Marigny nodded in answer, studying the trembling ancient where he lay. Atal's face was like a tiny wrinkled walnut; his head had a sparse crest of white hair; a long and voluminous beard like a fall of snow flowed down over the covers of his bed. And yet the eyes in the wrinkled face, faded as they were to the point of being colorless, had lit with an inner intelligence as they recognized the dreamer's lineage.

'Aye,' Atal continued, 'he came to see me once, your father, when first he entered dreamland to dwell here. A wise dreamer, and a fitting counselor to Randolph Carter. He came merely to see me, to honor me, but you –'

'I come to seek your help,' de Marigny promptly answered, 'in order to discover –'

'I know why you are here, my son,' Atal whispered. 'And I know who sent you. Am I not the high priest of the temple, and is this not the Temple of the Elder Ones? When the light of life flickers out in this old, old body, then it is my hope to move on to greater marvels, to immortality in Elysia, where I may continue to serve forever the elder Intelligences of my faith.' The old man paused to peer again at de Marigny where he stood by his bed. 'It is true that *They* sent you, those elder Beings, is it not?'

Once more de Marigny nodded, and when Atal spoke again his voice was very low, as if he wished to conceal his words even from the air of the room. 'Aye, I knew you were coming – you, instrument of Kthanid, great Voice of all the Gods of Eld – and I know where your friends are!'

'Titus Crow and Tiania?' De Marigny leaned closer, his eyes intent upon Atal's, aware of the ancient's fragile and trembling form.

Now it was Atal's turn to nod, and when he spoke again his voice was a low, fearful, broken whisper. 'They are on their way to Dylath-Leen, of which place I . . . I fear to speak. They are held prisoners of creatures whose very presence in dreamland is a blasphemy!'

'When will they get to Dylath-Leen? Is there a way I might intercept them en route? Who are these creatures that hold them captive, and where is Dylath –'

48

'I know much of Dylath-Leen.' Atal's dry whisper cut him off. 'But there is one who knows much more. He was once a dreamer, just like you, but now he is an inhabitant of Ulthar. He dwells here with his wife, two fine sons, and a daughter of great beauty. I can tell you where his house is – but, de Marigny –'

'Yes?'

'I have a feeling that time is running out quickly for your friends.' For a second or two the ancient's eyes seemed to gaze through the dreamer, as if they looked upon distant things, but then they focused upon him once more. 'Now you must eat. The food here at the temple is plain but wholesome. You are welcome to take a meal, but then you must be on your way. Please clap your hands for me; my own are not very strong.'

De Marigny clapped his hands once, and almost immediately one of the young priests entered the room. Atal told him to arrange a meal for their visitor, then lowered himself down once more onto his pillow. The audience was over.

Then, as the dreamer began to follow the young priest out of the room, Atal called out: 'Oh, de Marigny – I almost forgot. I have something for you, which you must take with you.' He reached beneath his pillow to take out a small, strangely shaped vial.

'It is a very potent liquid brewed here in Ulthar, in this very temple. Unknown in the waking world, and rare enough here in dreamland, it has the property of awakening dreamers from even the deepest slumbers. One sip will return a dreamer to the waking world in seconds – aye, and all he brought through the gates of dream with him. To the true inhabitant of dream, however, the potion is a deadly poison; for of course it "awakens" such inhabitants to a world in which they do not exist! It can be seen that they must quite simply . . . disappear.'

For a moment de Marigny looked stunned as the

49

implications dawned on him – then he cried out: 'What? A potion to awaken dreamers? Then I could take a sip right away, return to the time-clock, and then –'

'No, my young friend.' Atal held up a quieting hand. 'The potion is not yet quite ready. It has to ferment. I had it brewed as soon as I knew you were coming, for it came to me in a vision that you would need it. But you must wait for at least another day and a half a day before it will be safe to use. By that time, if good fortune goes with you, you ought to have found your friends.'

Later, as the first stars came out in the evening sky, de Marigny walked the cool streets of Ulthar to the house of Grant Enderby, late of the waking world. Enderby was the man who could tell him about Dylath-Leen, perhaps help him in his search for Titus Crow and Tiania.

Dylath-Leen . . . The very name conjured up strange pictures in the dreamer's mind, and as he walked the darkening streets and watched the lights coming on in friendly, small-paned windows, he wondered why Atal had been so loth to speak of the place. Well, before the night was out doubtless he would know well enough.

Following Atal's directions, de Marigny soon came to the path that led to Grant Enderby's house of red stone and dark oaken beams. And the red stone walls about the garden bore testimony to Enderby's calling here in dreamland, the fact that he was a quarrier, and his sons in his footsteps. The walls were broad and straight and strong, as was the man who built them.

And so the dreamer knocked upon the oaken door and was welcomed into the home of this one-time man of the waking world; and after his host's family were all to bed, de Marigny sat alone with Grant Enderby and listened until the wee hours to the following story . . .

Part Two

Grant Enderby's Story, I: Litha

Three times only have I visited basalt-towered, myriad-wharved Dylath-Leen, three curious visits which spanned almost a century of that city's existence. Now I am glad that I have seen it for the last time.

I went there first in my late teens, filled with a longing engendered of continuous study of such works as *The Arabian Nights* and Gelder's *Atlantis Found* for wondrous places of antique legend and fable and centuried cities of ages past. And my longing was not disappointed.

I first saw the city from afar, wandering along the river Skai with a caravan of merchants from distant places, and at first sight of the tall black towers which form the city's ramparts I felt a strange fascination for the place. Later, lost in awe and wonder, I took leave of my merchant friends to walk Dylath-Leen's ancient streets and alleys, to visit the wharfside taverns and chat with seamen from every part of Earth's dreamland – and with a few, I fancy, from more distant places.

I never once pondered my ability to chatter in their many tongues, for often things are far simpler in dream, nor did I wonder at the ease with which I fitted myself into the alien yet surprisingly friendly scene; once attired in robes of dream's styling, my looks were not unlike those of many of her peoples. I was a little taller than average, true, but in the main Dylath-Leen's diverse folk might well have passed for those of any town of the waking world, and vice versa.

Yet there were in the city others, strange traders from across the Southern Sea, whose appearance and *odor* filled me with a dread loathing so that I could not abide to stay near where they were for long. Of these traders and their origin I questioned the tavern-keepers, to be told that I was not the first from the waking world whose instinct found in those traders traces of hinted evil and deeds not to be mentioned. Randolph Carter himself had once warned Dylath-Leen's peoples that the traders were fiends not to be trusted, whose only desire was to spread horror and evil throughout all the lands of dream.

But when I heard Carter's name mentioned I was hushed, for an amateur at dreaming such as I was at that time could not dare aspire to walk even in the shadow of one such as he. Why, Carter was rumored to have been even to Kadath in the Cold Waste, to have confronted Nyarlathotep the Crawling Chaos, and to have returned unscathed from that place! How many could boast of that?

Yet loath though I was to have anything to do with those traders, I found myself one morning in the towering tavern of Potan-Lith, in a high barroom the windows of which looked out over the Bay of Wharves, waiting for the galley I had heard was coming to the city with a cargo of rubies from an unknown shore. I wanted to discover just what it was of them that so repelled me, and the best way to decide this, I thought, would be to observe them from a safe distant and location at which I, myself, might go unobserved. I did not wish to bring myself to the notice of those queerly frightening people of unguessed origin. Potan-Lith's tavern, with its ninety-nine steps, served my purpose admirably.

I could see the whole of the wharfside spread beneath me in the morning light; the nets of the fishermen drying, with smells of rope and deep ocean floating up to my window; the smaller craft of private tradesmen rolling gently at anchor, sails lowered and hatches laid back to

let the sun dry out their musty holds; the thag-weed merchants unloading their strongly-scented, dream-within-
dream-engendering opiates garnered in exotic Eastern
parts; and, eventually appearing on the horizon, the sails
of the black galley for which I so vigilantly waited. There
were other traders of the same race already in the city,
to be sure, but how could one get close to them without
attracting unwanted attention? My plan of observation
was best, I was certain, but I did not know just what it
was I wished to observe — or why.

It was not long before the black galley loomed against
the entrance of the bay. It slipped into the harbor past
the great basalt lighthouse, and a strange stench driven
by the South Wind came with it. As with the coming of
all such craft and their weird masters, uneasiness rippled
all along the waterfront as the silent ship closed with its
chosen wharf, and its three banks of briskly moving oars
stilled and slipped in through their oarlocks to the unseen
and equally silent rowers within. I watched eagerly then,
waiting for the galley's master and crew to come ashore,
but only five persons — if persons they truly were — chose
to leave that enigmatic craft. This was the best look at
such traders I had so far managed, and what I saw did
not please me at all.

I have intimated my doubts with regard to the humanity
of those — men? Let me explain why.

Firstly, their mouths were far too wide. Indeed, I
thought that one of them glanced up at my window
as he left the ship, smiling a smile which only just fell
within the boundaries of that word's limitations, and it
was horrible to see just how wide his evil mouth was.
Now what would any eater of normal foods want with
a mouth of such abnormal proportions? And for that
matter, why did the owners of such mouths wear such
queerly moulded turbans? Or was it simply the *way* in
which the turbans were worn? For they were humped up

55

in two points over the foreheads of the wearers in what seemed especially bad taste. And as for their shoes: well, they were certainly the most peculiar footwear I had ever seen, in or out of dreams. They were short, blunt-toed, and flat, as though the feet within were not feet at all! I thoughtfully finished off my mug of muth-dew and wedge of bread and cheese, turning from the window to leave the tavern of Potan-Lith.

My heart seemed to leap into my mouth. There in the low entrance stood that same merchant who had so evilly smiled up at my window! His turbaned head turned to follow my every move as I sidled out past him and flew down the ninety-nine steps to the wharf below. An awful fear pursued me as I ran through the alleys and streets, making my feet fly faster on the basalt flags of the wider pavements, until I reached the well known, green-cobbled courtyard wherein I had my room. But even there I could not get the face of that strangely turbaned, wide-mouthed trader from beyond the Southern Sea out of my mind, nor his smell from my nostrils. So I paid my landlord his due, moving out there and then to head for that side of Dylath-Leen which faces away from the sea and which is clean with the scents of window-box flowers and baking bread, where the men of the taverns rarely venture.

There, in the district called S'eemla, I found myself lodging with a family of basalt quarriers who were such good, cheerful, charming folk that later, when I became an inhabitant of dream proper, I too chose quarrying for my trade. The head of the house was named Bo-Kareth, and he provided me with my own wide-windowed garret room, with a bed and a mattress of fegg-down; so that soon it was as though I had been born into the family, or might have seemed had I been able to imagine myself a brother to comely Litha.

Within the month I was firmly settled in, and from then on I made it my business to carry on Randolph Carter's work of warning, putting in my word against the turbaned traders at every opportunity. My task was made no easier by the fact that I had nothing concrete to hold against them. There was only the feeling, already shared by many of the folk of Dylath-Leen, that trade between the city and the black galleys could bring to fruition nothing of any good.

Eventually my knowledge of the traders grew to include such evidences as to make me more certain than ever of their evil nature. Why should those black galleys come into harbor, discharge their four or five traders, and then simply lie there at anchor, emitting their foul odor, showing never a sign of their silent crews? That there were crews seems needless to state; with three great banks of oars to each ship there must have been many rowers. But what man could say just who or what such rowers were?

Too, the grocers and butchers of the city grumbled over the apparent frugality of those singularly shy crews, for the only things the traders bought with their great and small rubies were gold and stout Pargian slaves. This traffic had gone on for years, I was told, and in that time many a fat black man had vanished, never to be seen again, up the gangplanks into those mysterious galleys to be transported to lands across uncharted seas – if, indeed, such lands were their destination!

And where did the queer traders get their rubies, the like of which were to be found in no known mines in all Earth's dreamland? Yet those rubies came cheaply enough, too cheaply in fact, so that every home in Dylath-Leen contained them, some large enough to be used as paperweights in the homes of the richer merchants. Myself, I found those gems strangely loathsome, seeing in them only the reflections of the traders who brought them from across nameless oceans.

So it was that in the district called S'eemla my interest in the ruby traders waxed to its full, paled, waned, and finally withered – but never died completely. My new interest, however, in dark-eyed Litha, Bo-Kareth's daughter, grew with each passing day, and my nights were filled with dreams within dreams of Litha and her ways, so that only occasionally were my slumbers invaded by the unpleasantly-turbaned, wide-mouthed traders from unknown parts.

One evening, after a trip out to Ti-Penth, a village not far from Dylath-Leen where we enjoyed the annual Festival of Plenty, as Litha and I walked back hand in hand through the irrigated green valley called Tanta toward our black-towered city, she told me of her love and we sank together to the darkling sward. That night, when the city's myriad twinkling lights had all blinked out and the bats chittered thick without my window, Litha crept into my garret room and only the narg-oil lamp on the wall could tell of the wonders we knew with each other.

In the morning, rising rapidly in joy from my dreams within dreams, I broke through too many layers of that flimsy stuff which constitutes the world of the subconscious, to waken with a cry of agony in the house of my parents at Norden on the northeast coast. Thereafter I cried myself to sleep for a year before finally I managed to convince myself that my dark-eyed Litha existed only in dreams.

Grant Enderby's Story, II: The Ruby Horror

I was thirty years old before I saw Dylath-Leen again. I arrived in the evening, when the city was all but in darkness, but I recognized immediately the feel of those basalt flagstones beneath my feet, and, while the last of the myriad lights flickered out in the towers and the last tavern closed, my heart leaped as I turned my suddenly light feet toward the house of Bo-Kareth. But something did not seem right, and a horror grew rapidly upon me as I saw in the streets thickening groups of carousing, nastily chattering, strangely turbaned people not quite so much men as monsters. And many of them had had their turbans disarrayed in their sporting so that protuberances glimpsed previously only in books of witchcraft and the like and in certain biblical paintings showed clearly through! Once I was stopped and pawed vilely by a half-dozen of them. As they conferred over me in low, menacing tones, I tore myself free and fled. For they were indeed those same evil traders of yore, and I was horrified that they should be there in my City of Black Towers in such great numbers.

I must have seen hundreds of those vile creatures as I hurried through the city's thoroughfares; yet somehow I contrived to arrive at the house of Bo-Kareth without further pause or hindrance, and I hammered at his oaken door until a light flickered behind the round panes of blue glass in the upper sections of that entrance. It was Bo-Kareth himself who came to answer my banging, and he came wide-eyed with a fear I could well understand. Relief showed visibly in his whole aspect when he saw that only a man stood upon his step. Although he seemed amazingly *aged* – so aged, in fact, that I was taken aback (for I did not then know of the variations experienced by different dreamers, variations in the passage of time between the waking world and dreamland) – he recognized me at once, whispering my name:

'Grant! Grant Enderby! My friend – my old friend . . .! Come in, come in . . .'

'Bo-Kareth,' I burst out, 'Bo, I –'

'*Shhh!*' He pressed a finger to his lips, eyes widening even further than before, leaning out to glance up and down the street before pulling me in and quickly closing and bolting the door behind me. 'Quietly, Grant, quietly. This is a city of silence now, where *they* alone carouse and make their own hellish brand of merry – and they may soon be abroad and about their business.'

'*They?*' I questioned, instinctively knowing the answer.

'Those you once tried to warn us of. The turbaned traders.'

'I thought as much,' I answered. 'And they're already abroad, I've seen them. But what *business* is this you speak of?'

Then Bo-Kareth told me a tale that filled my heart with horror and determined me never to rest until I had at least attempted to right a great wrong.

It had started a number of years earlier, according to my host (I made no attempt to pinpoint a date; what was the point when Bo-Kareth had apparently aged thirty years to my twelve?) and had involved the bringing to the city of a gigantic ruby. This great gem had been a gift, an assurance of the traders' regard for Dylath-Leen's peoples, and as such had been set upon a pedestal in the city's main square. But only a few nights later the horror had started to make itself noticeable.

The keeper of a tavern near the square, peering from his window after locking the door for the night, had noticed a strange, deep, reddish glow from the giant gem's heart; a glow which seemed to pulse with an alien life all its own. And when the tavern-keeper told the next day of what he had seen an amazing thing came to light. All of the other galley-brought rubies in the city – the smaller gems set in rings, amulets, and instruments, and those larger, less ornamental, almost rude stones owned purely for the sake of ownership by certain of the city's richer gentlemen – had glowed through the night to a lesser degree, as if in response to the greater activity of their bulky brother. And with that unearthly glowing of the gems had come a strange partial paralysis, making all the peoples of the city other than the turbaned traders themselves slumberous and weak, incapable and unwanting of any festivity and barely able to go about their normal duties and business. As the days passed and the power of the great ruby and the less regal ones waxed, so also did the strange drowsiness upon Dylath-Leen's folks. And it was only then, too late, that the plot was seen and its purpose recognized.

For a long time there had been a shortage of the fat black slaves of Parg. They had been taken from the city by the traders faster than they came in, until only a handful remained; and that handful, on hearing one day of a black galley soon due to dock, had fled their masters and left the city to seek less suspicious bondage. That had been shortly before the horned traders brought the great jewel to Dyath-Leen, and since that time, as the leering, gem-induced lethargy had increased until its effects were felt in daylight almost as much as they were at night, so had the number of oddly-shod traders grown until the docks were full of their great black galleys.

Then, inexplicable absences began to be noticed; a taverner's daughter here and a quarrier there, a merchant from Ulthar and a thagweed curer and a silversmith's son. Soon any retaining sufficient willpower sold up their businesses, homes, and houses and left Dylath-Leen for Ti-Penth, Ulthar, and Nir. I was glad to learn that Litha and her brothers had thus departed, though it made me strangely sad to hear that when Litha went she took with her a handsome husband and two strong sons. She was old enough now, her father told me, to be mistaken for my mother; but she still retained her great beauty.

By this time the hour of midnight was well passed and all about the house tiny red points of light had begun to glow in an eerie, slumber-engendering coruscation. As

Bo-Kareth talked, his monologue interrupted now with many a yawn and shake of his head, I tracked down the sources of those weird points of radiance and found them to be rubies.

The curse was just as Bo-Kareth had described it – rubies! Ten tiny gems were set in the base of an ornamental goblet; many more of the small red stones enhanced the hanging silver and gold plates; fire-flashing splinters of precious crystal were embedded in the spines of certain of my host's leather-bound books of prayer and dream-lore – and when his mumbling had died away completely I turned from my investigations to find the old man asleep in his chair, lost in distressing dreams which pulled his gray face into an expression of muted terror.

I had to see the great gem. I make no excuse for such a rash and headstrong decision (one does things in dreams which one would never consider for a moment in the waking world) but I knew I could make no proper plans nor rest easy in my mind until I had seen that great ruby for myself.

I left the house by the back door, locking it behind me and pocketing the key. I knew Bo-Kareth had a duplicate key, and besides, I might later need to get into the house without delay. The layout of the city was well known to me, and thus it was not difficult for me to find my way through labyrinthine back streets to the main square. That square was away from the district of S'eemla, far closer to the docks and quays, and the nearer I drew to the waterfront the more carefully I crept.

Why, the whole area was alive with the alien and evil traders! The wonder is that I was not spotted in the first few minutes; and when I saw what those hellish creatures were up to, thus confirming beyond a shadow of a doubt Bo-Kareth's worst fears, the possibility that I might yet be discovered – and the consequences such an untimely discovery would bring – caused me to creep even more carefully. Each streetcorner became a focal point for terror, where lurking, unseen presences caused me to glance over my shoulder or jump at the slightest flutter of bat-wings or scurry of mice feet. And then, almost before I knew it, I came upon the square.

I came at a run, my feet flying frantically, all caution thrown to the wind. For I knew now for sure what the horned ones did at night, and a fancy had grown quickly on me that something followed in the dark; so that when I suddenly burst from that darkness into a blaze of red firelight I was taken completely by surprise. I literally keeled over backwards as I contrived to halt my flight of fear before it plunged me into the four turbaned terrors standing at the base of the dais of the jewel. My feet skidded as I pivoted on my heels and my fingers scrabbled madly at the round cobbles of the square as I fell. In truth it could scarce be termed a real fall – I was no sooner down than up – but in that split second or so as I fought to bring my careening body under control those guardians of the great gem were after me. Glancing fearfully back I saw them darting rat-like in my wake.

My exit from that square can only properly be described as panic-stricken, but brief though my visit had been I had seen more than enough to strengthen that first resolve of mine to do something about the loathsome and insidious invasion of the traders. Backtracking, bounding through the night streets I went, with the houses and taverns towering blackly on both sides, seeing in my mind's eye that horrible haunting picture which I had but glimpsed in the main square.

There had been the four guards with great knives fastened in their belts, the dais with pyramid steps to its flat summit, four hugely flaring torches in blackly-forged metal holders, and, atop the basalt altar itself, a great reddish mass pulsing with inner life, its myriad facets catching and reflecting the fire of the torches in a mixture with its own evil radiance. The hypnotic horror, the malignant monster – the great ruby!

Then the vision changed as I heard close behind me a weird, ululant cry – a definite *alert* – which carried and echoed in Dylath-Leen's canyon alleys. In rampant revulsion I pictured myself linked by an iron anklet to the long chain of mute, unprotesting people which I had seen only minutes earlier being led in the direction of the docks and the black galleys, and this monstrous mental image drove my feet to a frenzied activity that sent me speeding headlong down the dark passages between the city's basalt walls.

But fast and furious though my flight was, it soon became apparent that my pursuers were gaining on me. A faint padding came to my ears as I ran, causing me to accelerate, forcing my feet to pump even faster. The effort was useless, if anything, *worse* than useless, for I soon tired and had to slow down. Twice I stumbled and the second time, as I struggled to rise, the fumbling of slimy fingers at my feet lent them wings and shot me out again in front. It became as one of those nightmares (which indeed it was) where you run and run through vast vats of subconscious molasses, totally unable to increase the distance between yourself and your ethereal pursuer; the only difference being, dream or none, that I knew for a certainty I was running for my life!

It was a few moments later, when an added horror had just about brought me to the verge of giving up hope, that I found an unexpected but welcome reprieve. Slipping and stumbling, panting for air, I had been brought up short by a mad fancy that the soft padding of alien feet now came from the very direction in which I was heading, from somewhere in *front* of me! And as those sounds of demon footfalls came closer, closing in on me, I flattened myself to the basalt wall, spreading my arms and groping desperately with my hands at the bare, rough stone; and there, beneath my unbelieving fingers – *an opening!* – a narrow crack or entry, completely hidden in jet shadows, between two of the street's bleak buildings.

I squeezed myself into the narrow opening, trying to get my breathing under control, fighting a lunatic urge to cry out in my terror. It was pitch black, the blackness of the pit, and a hideous thought suddenly came to me. What if this tunnel of darkness – this possible gateway to sanity – what if it were closed, a dead end? That would be a dead end indeed! Then, as if in answer to my silent, frantic prayers, even as I heard the first squawk of amazed frustration from somewhere behind me, I squirmed from the other end of the division to emerge in a street mercifully void of the evil aliens.

My flight had carried me in a direction well away from Bo-Kareth's house; but in any case, now that my worst fears were realized and the alarm raised, it would have been completely idiotic to think of hiding anywhere in the city. I had to get away, to Ulthar or Nir, as far as possible – and as fast as possible – until I could try to find a way to rid Dylath-Leen of its inhuman curse.

Less than an hour later, with the city behind me, I was in an uninhabited desert area heading in a direction which I hoped would eventually bring me to Ulthar. It was cool beneath a full, cloud-floating moon, yet a long while passed before the fever of my panic-flight left me. When it did I was almost sorry, for soon I found myself shivering as the sweat of my body turned icy chill, and I wrapped my cloak more tightly about me for I knew it must grow still colder before the dawn. I was not particularly worried about food or water; there are many water holes and oases between Dylath-Leen and Ulthar. No, my main cause for concern lay in orientation. I did not want to end up wandering in one of the many great parched deserts! My sense of direction in open country has never been very good.

Before long, great clouds came drifting in from a direction I took to be the south, obscuring the moon until only the stars in the sky ahead gave any light by which to travel. Then, it seemed, the dune-cast shadows grew blacker and longer and an eerie sensation of not being alone waxed in me. I found myself casting sharp, nervous glances over my shoulder and shuddering to an extent not entirely warranted by the chill of the night. There grew in my mind an awful suspicion, one which I had to resolve one way or the other.

I hid behind a dune and waited, peering back the way I had come. Soon I saw a darting shadow moving swiftly over the sand, following my trail – and that shadow was endowed with twin points at its top and chuckled obscenely as it came. My hair stood on end as I saw the creature stop to study the ground, then lift its wide-mouthed face to the night sky. I heard again that weird, ululant cry of alert – and I waited no longer.

In a passion of fear even greater than that which I had known in the streets of Dylath-Leen, I fled – racing like a madman over the night sands, scrambling and often falling head over heels down the sides of the steeper sandhills, until my head struck something hard in the shadow of a dune and I was knocked unconscious.

But it seems that I was not too deeply gone in dream to be shocked back into the waking world, and I was fortunate enough to wake up before my pursuer could find me. This time I was far from sorry when I leapt shouting awake at my home in Norden; and in the sanity of the waking world I recognized the fact that all those horrors of dream and the night had existed only in my slumbers, so that in the space of a few days my second visit to Dylath-Leen was all but forgotten. The mind soon forgets that which it cannot bear to remember . . .

Grant Enderby's Story, III:
The Utterer of the Words

I was forty-seven when next – when last – I saw Dylath-Leen. Not that my dream took me straight to the basalt city; rather, I found myself first on the outskirts of Ulthar, the City of Cats. Wandering through the city's streets, I stooped to pet a fat tom as he lazed upon a doorstep, and an old shopkeeper seated outside his store beneath a shade called out to me in a friendly, quavering voice:

'It is good, stranger. It is good when a stranger pets the cats of Ulthar. Have you journeyed far?'

'Far,' I affirmed. 'From the waking world. But even there I stop to play when I see a cat. Tell me, sir, can you direct me to the house of Litha, daughter of Bo-Kareth of Dylath-Leen?'

'Indeed, I know her well.' He nodded his old head. 'She is one of the few in Ulthar with as many years to count as I. She lives with her husband and family not far from here. Until some years ago her father also lived at his daughter's house. He came out of Dylath-Leen mazed and mumbling, and did not live long here in Ulthar. Now no man goes to Dylath-Leen.'

But the old man had soured at the thought of Dylath-Leen and did not wish to talk any longer. I took his directions and started off with mixed feelings along the street he had indicated; but only halfway up that street I cut off down a dusty alley and made for the Temple of the Elder Ones instead. It could do no good to see Litha now. What use to wake old memories – if indeed she were capable of remembering anything of those golden days of her youth? And it was not as though she might help me solve my problem.

That same problem of thirteen waking years ago: how to

avenge the outraged peoples of Dylath-Leen, and how to rescue those of them – if any such existed – still enslaved. For there was still a feeling of yearning in me for the black-towered city and its peoples of yore. I remembered the friends I had known and my many walks through the high-walled streets and along the farm lanes of the outskirts. Yet even in S'eemla the knowledge that certain offensive black galleys were moored in the docks had somehow always sufficed to dull my appetite for living, had even impaired the happiness I had known with dark-eyed Litha, in the garret of Bo-Kareth's house, with the bats of night clustered thick and chittering beneath the sill without my window.

As quickly as the vision of Litha the girl came, I put it out of my mind, striding out more purposefully for the Temple of the Elder Ones. If any man could help me in my bid for vengeance against the turbaned traders, Atal, the Priest of the Temple, was that man. It was rumored that in the temple he had keep of many incredible volumes of sorcery. His great knowledge of the darker mysteries was, in fact, my main reason for seeking his aid. I could hardly hope to engage the forces of evil controlled by the hell-traders with physical means alone.

It was then, as I left the little green cottages and neatly fenced farms and shady shops of the suburbs behind me, as I pressed more truly into the city proper, that I received a shock so powerful my soul almost withered within me. It is a wonder that I was not driven to seek refuge in the waking world, but a vision of vengeance made me cling desperately to dreamland.

I had allowed myself to become interested in the old peaked roofs, the overhanging upper storeys, numberless chimney pots, and narrow, old cobbled streets of the city, so that my attention had been diverted from the path my feet followed, causing me to bump rudely into someone coming out of the narrow door of a shop. Of a sudden the air was foul with shuddersome, well remembered odors of hideous connection, and my hackles rose as I backed quickly away from the strangely turbaned, squat figure I had chanced into. The slightly tilted eyes regarded me curiously and a wicked smile played around the too wide mouth.

One of *Them!* Here in Ulthar?

I mumbled incoherent apologies, slipped past the still evilly grinning figure, and ran the rest of the way to the Temple of the Elder Ones. If there had been any suggestion of half-heartedness to my intentions earlier there was certainly none now! It seemed obvious to me the course events were taking. First it had been Dylath-Leen, now an attempt at Ulthar. Where next? Nowhere, if I had anything to say of it.

I found the patriarch I sought, Atal of Hatheg-Kla, Atal the Ancient, in the Room of Ancient Records low in the great tower that houses the Temple of the Elder Ones. He sat, in flowing black and gold robes, at a centuried wooden bench, fading eyes studiously lost in the yellowed pages of a great aeon-worn book, its metal hasps dully agleam in a stray beam of sunlight striking in from the single high window.

He looked up, starting as if in shock as I entered the musty room with its tall bookshelves. Then he pushed his book away and spoke:

'The Priest of the Temple greets you, stranger. You *are* a stranger, are you not?'

'I have seen Ulthar before,' I answered. 'But, yes, I am a stranger here in the Temple of the Elder Ones. I come from the waking world, Atal, to seek your help.'

'Huh!' He was calmer now. 'You are not the first from the waking world to ask my aid, nor the last I fancy. How are you named and in what manner might I assist you? – *if* I choose to assist you!'

'My name is Grant Enderby, Atal, and the help I as[k]
is not for myself. I come in the hope that you might b[e]
able to help me rid Dylath-Leen of a certain contagion[,]
but since coming to Ulthar today I have learned that eve[n]
here the sores are spreading. Are there not even now i[n]
Ulthar strange traders from no clearly named land? Is i[t]
not so?'

'It is so.' He nodded his venerable head. 'Say on.'

'Then you should know that they are those same trader[s]
who brought Dylath-Leen to slavery – an evil, hypnoti[c]
slavery – and I fancy that they mean to use the same blac[k]
arts here in Ulthar to a like end. Do they trade rubies th[e]
like of which are found in no known mine in the whole o[f]
dreamland?'

Again he nodded: 'They do – but say no more. I a[m]
already aware. At this very moment I search for a mean[s]
by which the trouble may be put to an end. But I wor[k]
only on rumors, and I am unable to leave the temple t[o]
verify those rumors. My duties are all important, and i[n]
any case, these bones are too old to wander very far . . .[']
He paused for a moment, then continued.

'Truly, Dylath-Leen did suffer an evil fate, but thin[k]
not that her peoples had no warning. Why, even a centur[y]
ago the city's reputation was bad, through the presence o[f]
those very traders you have mentioned. Another dreame[r]
before you saw the doom in store for the city, speakin[g]
against those traders vehemently and often; but his word[s]
were soon forgotten by all who heard them and peopl[e]
went their old ways as of yore. No man may help hi[m]
who will not help himself.

'But it is the presence of those traders here in Ultha[r]
which has driven me to this search of mine. I cannot allo[w]
the same doom to strike here – whatever that doom ma[y]
be – yet it is difficult to see what may be done. No ma[n]
of this town will venture anywhere near Dylath-Leen. I[t]
is said that the streets of that city have known no huma[n]

feet for more than twenty years, nor can any man say with any certainty where the city's peoples have gone.'

'I can say!' I answered. 'Not *where*, exactly, but *how* at least. Enslaved, I said, and told no lie. I had it first from Bo-Kareth, late of Dylath-Leen, who told me that when those traders had taken all the fat black slaves of Parg for those evil stones of theirs, they brought to the city the biggest ruby ever seen – a boulder of a gem – leaving it on a pedestal in the main square as a false token of esteem. It was the evil influence of this great jewel that bewitched the people of Dylath-Leen, bemusing them to such a degree that in the end they, too, became slaves to be led away to the black galleys of the traders. And now, apparently, those traders have . . . *used up* . . . all the peoples of that ill-omened city and are starting their monstrous game here! And Bo-Kareth's story was true in every detail, for with my own eyes –'

'A great ruby . . . hmmm!' Atal musingly cut me off, stroking his face and frowning in concentration. 'That puts a different complexion on it. Yes, I believe that in the *Fourth Book* there may be a mention! Shall we see?'

I nodded my eager agreement, and at Atal's direction lifted down from a corner shelf the largest and weightiest tome I had ever seen. Each page – pages of no material I had ever known before – glowed with burning letters which stood out with firefly definition in the dimness of the room. I could make out nothing of the unique ciphers within the book, but Atal seemed thoroughly familiar with each alien character, translating easily, mumbling to himself in barely discernible tones, until suddenly he stopped. He lurched shakily to his feet then, slamming the priceless volume shut, horror burning in his ancient eyes.

'So!' he exclaimed, hissing out the word. 'It is *that!* The Fly-the-Light from Yuggoth on the Rim, a vampire in the worst meaning of the word – and we must make sure that it is never brought to Ulthar!' He paused, visibly taking hold of himself before he could continue.

'Let me tell you:

'Long ago, before dreams, in the primal mist of the predawn Beginning of All, the great ruby was brought from distant Yuggoth on the Rim by the Old Ones. Within that jewel, prisoned by light and the magic of the Old Ones, lurks a basic avatar of the prime evil, a thing hideous as the pit itself! Understand, Grant Enderby, it is not the stone that induces the hypnotic weariness of which you have spoken, but the thing *within* the stone, the evil influence of the Fly-the-Light from dark Yuggoth on the Rim. Few men know the history of that huge jewel and its monstrous inhabitant, and I do not consider myself fortunate to be one of the few.

'It is told that it was discovered after coming down in an avalanche from the heights of forbidden Hatheg-Kla – which I can believe for I know much of that mountain – discovered and carried away by the Black Princess, Yath-Lhi of Tyrhhia. And when her caravan reached her silver-spired city it was found that all Yath-Lhi's men at arms, her slaves, even the Black Princess herself, were as zombies, altered and mazed. It is not remembered now where Tyrhhia once stood, but many believe the centuried desert sands to cover even its tallest spire, and that the remains of its habitants lie putrid within their buried houses.

'But the ruby was not buried with Tyrhhia, more's the pity, and rumor has it that it was next discovered in a golden galley on the Southern Sea twixt Dylath-Leen and the Isle of Oriab. A strange ocean is the Southern Sea, and especially between Oriab and Dylath-Leen; for there, many fathoms deep, lies a basalt city with a temple and monolithic altar. And sailors are loth to pass over that submarine city, fearing the great storms which legend has it strike suddenly, even when there is no breath of wind to stir the sails!

'However, there the great jewel was found, aboard a great golden galley, and the crew of that galley were very beautiful even though they were not men, and all were long dead but not corrupt! Only one sailor, mad and babbling, was later rescued from the sea off Oriab to gibber pitifully the tale of the golden galley, but of his fellow crewmates nothing more is known. It is interesting to note that it is further writ how only certain people – horned people who dance to the evil drone of pipes and the rattle of crotala in mysterious Leng – are unaffected by the stone's proximity!' Atal looked at me knowingly. 'And I can see you have already noticed how strangely our traders wear their turbans . . .

'But I digress. Again the jewel survived whatever fate overtook the poor seamen who rescued it from the golden galley, and it was later worshiped by the enormous dholes in the Vale of Pnoth, until three leathery night-gaunts flew off with it over the Peaks of Throk and down into those places of subterranean horror of which certain dim myths hint most terribly. For that underworld is said to be a place litten only by pale death-fires, a place reeking of ghoulish odours and filled with the primal mists which swirl in the pits at Earth's core. Who may say what form the inhabitants of such a place might take?'

At this point Atal's eyes cleared of their faraway look and turned from the dark places of his tale to the present and to me. He placed his rheumy hands on my shoulders, peering at me earnestly.

'Well, so says legend and the *Fourth Book of D'harsis* – and now, you say, the great ruby is come again into the known places of Earth's dreamland. I believe it, for over the years there have been vague rumors. Now hear you, Grant Enderby, I know what must be done – but how may I ask any man to take such risks? For my plan involves not only the risk of destruction to the mortal body, but the possible eternal damnation of the immortal soul!'

73

'I have pledged myself,' I told him, 'to avenge the peoples of Dylath-Leen. My pledge still stands, for though Dylath-Leen is lost, yet are there other towns and cities in dreams which I would dream again – but not to see them corrupted by horned horrors that trade in fever-cursed rubies! Atal – tell me what I must do.'

Atal then set himself to it, and there was much for him to be about. I could not help him with the greater part of his work, tasks involving the translation into language I could understand of certain tracts from the *Fourth Book of D'harsis*. Even though many things are simpler in dream, those passages were not meant to be read by any man, neither awake nor sleeping, who did not understand their importance.

Slowly but surely the hours passed, and Atal labored as I watched, putting down letter after letter in the creation of pronounceable syllables from the seemingly impossible mumbo-jumbo of the great book from which he drew. I began to recognize certain symbols I had seen in allegedly 'forbidden' tomes in the waking world, and even began to mumble the first of them aloud – '*Tetragammaton Thabaite Sabaoth Tethiktos*' – until Atal silenced me by jerking to his feet and favoring me with a gaze of pure horror.

'It is almost night,' he remonstrated, striking a flint to a wax candle, his hands shaking more than even his extreme age might reasonably explain, 'and outside the shadows are lengthening. Would you call *That* forth without first having protection? For make no mistake, distance is of no consequence to this invocation, and if we wished we could call out the Fly-the-Light even from here. But first you must cast a spell over Dylath-Leen, to contain the thing when you release it from the ruby; for certainly unless it is contained it will ravish the whole of dreamland. And you, the caller, the Utterer of The Words, would be one of the first to die – horribly!'

I gulped my apologies and sat silently from then on, listening attentively to Atal's instructions even as my eyes followed his scratching pen.

'You must go to Dylath-Leen,' he told me, 'taking with you the two incantations I now prepare. One of them, which you will keep at your left, is to build the protective Wall of Naach-Tith about the city. To work this spell you must journey around Dylath-Leen, returning to your starting point and crossing it, chanting the words as you go. This means, of course, that you will need to cross the bay; and I suggest that you do this by boat, for there are things in the night sea that do not take kindly to swimmers.

'When you have crossed your starting point the wall will be builded. Then you may use the other chant, spoken only once, to shatter the great gem. You should carry the second chant at your right. This way you will not confuse the two – a mistake which would prove disastrous! I have used inks which shine in the dark; there will be no difficulty in reading the chants. So, having done all I have told you, your revenge will be complete and you will have served all the lands of dream greatly.

'No creature or thing will ever be able to enter Dylath-Leen again so long as the Wall of Naach-Tith is there, nor leave the place, and the Fly-the-Light will be loosed amongst the horned ones. One warning though, Grant Enderby – *do not watch the results of your work!* It will be as was never meant for the eyes of men.'

Grant Enderby's Story, IV: The Wall of Naach-Tith

I came through the desert toward Dylath-Leen at dusk, when the desert grasses made spiky silhouettes atop the dunes and the last kites circled high, their shrill cries telling of night's stealthy approach. Night was indeed coming, striding across dreamland in lengthening shadows which befriended and hid me as I tethered my yak and made for the western point of the bay. I would start there, making my way from shadow to shadow with the wall-building Chant of Naach-Tith on my lips, to the opposite side of the bay; and then I would see about crossing the water back to my starting point.

I was glad that the moon was thinly-horned, glad the desert was not more brightly illumined, for I could not be sure that there were no sentries out from the unquiet city. Whatever joys Dylath-Leen may once have held for me, now the place was unquiet. No normal lights shone in its streets and squares; but, as night came more quickly, there soon sprang up many thousands of tiny points of evil red, and in one certain area a great morbidly red blotch glowed in strange reminiscence of Jupiter's huge eye-like spot, glimpsed often in my youth through a friend's telescope. Empty though the city now was of all normal life, that poisoned jewel in the main square still filled the town with its loathsomeness, a terror ignored by the abnormal traders as the statues of past heroes are ignored in saner places.

Halfway round the city's perimeter there came to my ears the strains of music – if such evilly soul-disturbing sounds warrant placing in any such category – and leaping fires sprang up in Dylath-Leen's outer streets, so that I could see and shudder at the horned figures that leapt and cavorted round those ritual hellfires, observing disgustedly the way their squat bodies jerked and shook to the jarring cacophony of bone-dry crotala and strangled flutes. I could neither bear to hear nor watch, and so passed quickly on, chanting breathlessly to myself and feeling about me a weird magic building up to a thrill of unseen energies in the night air.

I was more than three-quarters towards the eastern side of the bay when I heard far behind me a sound that stiffened the short hairs on the back of my neck and brought a chill sweat to my brow. It was the terrified cry of my yak, and following that single shrill scream of animal fear there came another sound – one which caused me to quicken my pace almost to a run as I emerged from the dunes to the washed pebbles of the shore – the horrid, ululant cry of alarm of the horned ones!

Stranded on the beach, its bottom festooned with barnacles, was a small one-man craft as used of old by the octopus fishers of Dylath-Leen. Frail and unsafe though this vessel looked, beggars cannot be choosers, and thus thinking I leapt within its tar-planked shell, offering up a prayer of thanks to the night skies when I found that the craft still floated. I found the old round-bladed paddle and, still chanting those mad words of Atal's deciphering, made strongly for the black outline of the far side of the bay. And, ungainly though my craft had at first looked, it fairly cleft the dark water as I drove furiously at the paddle.

By now there were squattish outlines on the shore behind me, dancing in anger at my escape to the sea, and I wondered if the horned ones had a means of communication with which more orthodox creatures such as men were unfamiliar. If so, then perhaps I would find monstrous welcomers awaiting my beaching on the western point.

Halfway across the bay things happened to make me forget the problem of what might wait for me on landing. I felt a tug at my paddle from the oily water and a dark mass rose up out of the depths before my boat. As that unknown swimmer came alongside and the thin moonlight lit on its sharp teeth, I lashed out with my paddle – taking a very deep breath when the horror turned slowly away and silently submerged.

I continued then with my frenzied paddling and chanting until the western point loomed out of the dark and the shallow keel of my boat bit sand. Leaping overboard into shallow, night-chilled water, I imagined soggy gropings at my legs and ploughed in an agony of terror for the pebbles of the beach – and in that same instant, as I touched dry land, there loped out of the dark from the direction of the city the squat forms of a dozen or so of those foul, horned creatures whose brothers dwell in nighted Leng! Before they could reach me, even as their poisonous paws stretched out for me, I raced across my starting point and there came a clap of magical thunder that hurled me down face first into the sand. I leapt up again, and there within arm's length, clawing at an unseen barrier – the merciful Wall of Naach-Tith – were those thwarted horned ones of elder dreams. Hateful their looks and murderous their strangled intent as they clawed with vile purpose at thin air, held back by the invisible spell of Naach-Tith's barrier.

Without pause I snatched out the second of those papers given me by Atal and commenced the invocation of the Fly-the-Light, the spell to draw forth the horror from the ruby. And as the first of those weird syllables passed my lips the horned ones fell back, unbelievable terror twisting their already awful features.

'*Tetragammaton Thabaite Sabaoth Tethiktos –*' As I chanted on, by the dim light of that thin-horned moon the snarls of those creatures at bay turned to pleading mewls and gibbers as they began to grovel at the base of the Wall of Naach-Tith. And eventually I spoke the last rune, and there came a silence which was as that quiet that rules at the core of the moon.

Then, out of the silence, a low and distant rumble was born, growing rapidly in volume to a roar, to a blast of sound, to an ear-splitting shriek as of a billion banshees – and from the heart of Dylath-Leen a cold wind blew extinguishing in an instant the hellfires of the horned ones. And all the tiny red points of light went out in a second, and there came a loud, sharp crack, as of a great crystal disintegrating. And soon thereafter I heard the first of the screams.

I remembered Atal's warning 'not to watch,' but found myself unable to turn away. I was rooted to the spot, and as the screams from the dark city rose in unbearable intensity I could but stare into the darkness with bulging eyes, straining to pick out some detail of what occurred there in the midnight streets. Then, as the grovelers at the wall broke and scattered, *It* came!

It came – rushing from out the bowels of the terrified town – bringing with it a wind that bowled over the fleeing creatures beyond the invisible wall as though they had no weight at all . . . and I *saw* it!

Blind and yet all-seeing – without legs and yet running like flood water – the poisonous mouths in the bubbling mass – the Fly-the-Light beyond the wall. Great God! The sight of the creature was mind-blasting! And what it *did* to those now pitiful things from Leng. . . .

Thus it was.

Three times only have I visited the basalt-towered, myriad-wharved city of Dylath-Leen – and now I am glad that I have seen that city for the last time.

Part Three

1

Shadow Over Dreamland

'And it is still your intention to enter Dylath-Leen? Deliberately, despite all I have told you?' Grant Enderby's voice showed his incredulity. He stood up to pace the floor of the room wherein he and Henri-Laurent de Marigny had so firmly cemented their friendship through the hours of darkness. Enderby's tale had taken until the wee hours in the telling, and since then the two men had talked of a variety of things. Their discourse had covered many subjects, some of them centering upon de Marigny's quest, others touching upon the general air of malaise, of a strange impending doom that seemed to hang like a dark shadow over most of dreamland.

'Yes,' de Marigny answered, 'I must enter Dylath-Leen; my friends are there and they are in trouble.'

'But, Henri, if the Elder Gods themselves are incapable of helping your friends, then what can a mere man do?'

'You ask me that? And you, a "mere man," once built the Wall of Naach-Tith about Dylath-Leen, destroying all of the horned traders in the city.'

'I was lucky,' the older man grunted. 'Without Atal's help I could have done nothing.'

'But I, too, have been helped by Atal,' de Marigny pointed out. 'And I have my flying cloak.'

'Huh!' Enderby grunted grudgingly. 'Still, you do not know what you go against, Henri.'

'Oh, but I do. You have told me what I go against, Grant, for which I am grateful. There is something further, however.'

'Oh?'

'Yes. You explained how you built the Wall of Naach-Tith about Dylath-Leen, but you said nothing about its removal. How can you be sure that things are once more as they were — that Dylath-Leen again suffers the contagion of the horned traders?'

Enderby shrugged. 'There are reasons. Travelers have strayed too close to the city, never to be seen again; others have been lucky enough to escape. It is rumored that two such men have stumbled away from the city in the last five years, two out of dozens lost forever. Then there is the vision you saw in Kthanid's crystal: the square in the center of Dylath-Leen, where once again the horned ones have set up a great ruby which doubtless pulses out its evil, debilitating radiations even now . . .

'As to how the horned ones regained Dylath-Leen — how they chained the Fly-the-Light from Yuggoth on the Rim, prisoning it again within this new ruby they have brought to the city from across the Southern Sea — of these things I can only guess. And anyone's guess is as good as mine. Remember, Henri, that there was a rune to build the Wall of Naach-Tith, and another to splinter the great ruby and free the Fly-the-Light. Why not a third to remove Naach-Tith's barrier, and yet another to prison the horror from Yuggoth?

'It is after all a Fly-the-Light, which, during the hours of day, must find a dark sanctuary or perish beneath the sun's rays. If man — or monster — knew the correct runes, it would be an easy task to trap the vampire during the hours of daylight.'

Wearily de Marigny stroked his forehead. 'Whichever way it is,' he answered, 'I'll find out soon enough for myself.' He stood up and stretched, and his host immediately apologized.

'I fear I've kept you up talking too long, my friend. Let me show you to your room now. You have come a long way and will probably need all the strength you can muster. When will you tackle Dylath-Leen?'

Following Enderby upstairs to the tiny guestroom, de Marigny answered. 'I intend it to be tomorrow night, and of course I will fly into the city. That way the journey will be one of minutes, a half hour at most. With luck I should be in and out of Dylath-Leen before your horned traders even suspect that I am there. I won't need much more equipment than I have already: a rope – a sharp knife, perhaps – a little blacking for my face.'

'Ah, well, Henri, go to your bed now,' his host answered. 'We'll talk again tomorrow, when you are fully rested. If only I were a young man again, I –'

'No, no – you've done enough already, Grant, and I am extremely grateful.'

'My boys, too,' Enderby nodded, ushering the man from the waking world into the guestroom. 'If you were going afoot, I would find it difficult to dissuade them from going with you. You will understand why I am glad you are flying to Dylath-Leen.'

De Marigny nodded. 'Of course I understand, but in any case it's best I go it alone. Goodnight, Grant.'

'Goodnight, my friend. And may your dreams within dreams be pleasant ones.'

The following evening, as twilight deepened and the first suggestions of stars began to glow dimly in the sky over Ulthar, de Marigny set out. People who saw his shadow and the shape that cast it flitting high over the rooftops would later talk of a great bat; or perhaps it was a night-gaunt – though night-gaunts were extremely rare in these parts.

As the dreamer passed swiftly through the darkening sky he retraced in his mind's eye the comprehensive map of Dylath-Leen which Grant Enderby had drawn for him. It was of the utmost importance that he remember all of the routes from the square of the ruby dais to the outskirts of the city, and from the outskirts to the desert. It would not be too difficult to reach that square, where by now Titus Crow and Tiania might well be suffering the none too tender attentions of the squat horned ones. But it could very well be a different story again to escape from the place.

De Marigny had upon his person a stout rope with a noose, a sharp knife in a leather sheath, and the precious vial given him by Atal. Nothing more. He hoped that nothing more would be necessary, for he dared not weigh himself down too much.

Out in the desert he paused briefly to alight and tie his rope to a boulder that must have weighed as heavy as two men. With the other end of the rope fastened to the harness of his cloak, he attempted an ascent into the night. His spirits dropped when, as he had feared, he found the cloak incapable of lifting the additional weight. He found a second boulder only half so great as the first and repeated the experiment, feeling a little of his confidence returning as the cloak bore its burden slowly but surely up into dark skies.

The cloak could manage two people without being taxed beyond its capabilities, but not three. That was more or less as de Marigny had expected, but he had hoped –

No, he checked himself, hope was nothing without strength and determination. He untied the smaller boulder and wound the rope about his body once more. Then, slitting his eyes against a wind that blew high above the desert, following the winding course of a river of stars reflected in the night-dark Skai, he once more headed for Dylath-Leen.

Fires surrounded the city, spaced out to form a horse-shoe pattern whose mouth was the bay of Dylath-Leen, where the land met the currents of the Southern Sea. Seeing these fires from afar, de Marigny rose higher in the sky until he could plainly make out the shape they formed. Then he flew up higher still so that there could be no chance of his being observed as he soared above the watchers who kept those fires burning.

There were other lights in the city, but they were not the healthy, welcoming lights of any normal town. There was no physical warmth in them for all their redness, and de Marigny knew that these crimson glow-worms were only smaller versions of the great malignancy in the central square, the horror which even now pulsed out its red rays, glowing like the evil eye of an alien Cyclops. And seeing from on high that great unwinking glow, de Marigny believed he knew now for sure the source of all the unease in dreamland.

2

Rescue

To the three squat creatures whose task it was to guard the two dreaming humans spreadeagled upon the steps of the ruby dais, the night was a welcome, beautiful thing. Most of their fellows were asleep now, for there were no longer any of the normal inhabitants of dreamland left in Dylath-Leen with which to amuse themselves. It had been thus for many a year, unless one cared to count the occasional unwary wanderer who might stumble mistakenly upon Dylath-Leen from out of the desert. This night, however, should prove a rare diversion – in the shapes of these two very important intruders from the waking world of men.

The grotesquely alien trio that formed the nightguard about the dais of the ruby would have to be patient, though, waiting until they could be sure that they would not be disturbed in their pleasures. Lots had been drawn for their 'duty' this night, and the trio had been the winners. The prize must surely be enjoyed to the full, and it would be a pity if the cries of these two captives should attract jealous-minded colleagues to spoil their amusements.

The male captive would provide hours of sport, though he must not be *too* severely damaged. Nyarlathotep, emissary of Great Cthulhu himself, was coming to dreamland to speak with Titus Crow personally. It would not be meet if the Crawling Chaos should find the man a babbling idiot before he could question him – though doubtless he would be just such an idiot by the time the interrogation was over! As for the female . . . Ah! But *there* was a thought . . . They would have her one at a time, right there upon the dais steps, where her male companion could see and hear all that occurred. And later, before the morrow, they would have her again, perhaps all three at once!

As night deepened and the city grew quieter still, the three horned ones joked of such things and ensured that their captives overheard them – never knowing that upon a high, nearby rooftop a third party also heard them, nor that the unseen stranger grew livid with rage at their vileness!

The figures of the two captives tied to the dais steps were pitiful in their helplessness. Titus Crow, normally so proud and leonine – with eyes that spoke the secrets of strange ways walked unafraid, a man whose deeds had rocked the seats of the Great Old Ones themselves before taking him to the home of the Elder Gods in Elysia – now lay like a man already dead, naked and ready for the shroud. The ridges of the basalt steps bruised his back and cut into his flesh; his head lolled drunkenly; the only spark glowing behind his eyes was one of horror and shame. Shame that he was helpless now to protect the incredibly beautiful girl-goddess whose love for him had led her to this hideous place, this unthinkable fate.

The two gazed at each other, and for a moment their love blazed through all the misery. 'Oh, Titus,' the wondrous girl's equally wondrous voice, weak now and terrified, spoke to her Earthman. 'Is this really how it is all to end?'

'Tiania,' Crow's own voice plumbed the depths of wretchedness and shame, 'I would not have –'

'Hush, my Titus,' she shook her head, 'for I would have it no other way. If we are to suffer and die, then we suffer and die together. Do you think I would even want to live without you?'

Before Crow could answer, the rattling, rasping tones of one of the squat, alien guardsmen crackled harshly in the still air. 'Hah! The two lovers converse! See how they gaze upon one another and mumble their sweet nothings!' The speaker turned to his comrades. 'What do you say, brothers? Is it not time we found ourselves a morsel of pleasure with these two?'

'Indeed,' one of the two he addressed grated impatiently, 'if you two had listened to me we'd have been at it an hour ago. I want the girl – and I want her now!' The great wide mouth in the speaker's evil face widened even further in a ghastly grin as he stared at the writhing figure of Tiania upon the basalt steps.

Hearing this horned one's words, Titus Crow struggled wretchedly, helplessly with his bonds, gasping: 'By God, I'll –'

'You'll what, dreamer?' With his scimitar, the same horned one carelessly drew a thin red line down Crow's rib cage.

'Hold!' cried the third of the aliens. He approached Tiania and reached out a vile paw to snatch away the tattered square of silk which alone covered her perfect breasts. 'We haven't yet decided who's to be first with the girl, have we?' He took from his belt a pouch, and from this removed a ten-sided die. 'Highest score takes her first, lowest last. Agreed?'

His two companions nodded, at which he flipped his gamestone into the air. It fell, bounced, and the three horned ones crowded about it where it lay. 'Ten!' crowed the thrower, delighted with his luck.

The next guardsman threw only a four, at which he grunted a low curse. But the third also threw a ten. To break the tie, the first thrower took up the die a second time, at which his opponent said:

'Throw it higher this time. I don't trust you and your die.'

'High as you like,' chortled the other, flinging the gamestone into the air. It did not return to earth.

The three looked up into the night for a little while, shading their eyes against the lurid glow of the great ruby, then peered puzzledly at each other and frowned uncertainly. And in this moment of indecision a noose snaked down out of darkness and settled about the shoulders of the lost gamestone's owner.

The noose swiftly lifted and tightened about the guardsman's fat neck, drawing him inexorably up from the ground. He disappeared into the sky, choking and gurgling and kicking wildly. Stunned, his companions gaped at one another – for a second or two only. Then, before they could make a move, the now inert body of their hanged comrade crashed down again from a great height, dashing one of the two remaining horrors to the ground with a broken back.

At that, the legs of the third member of that loathsome trio were galvanized into frantic activity. It seemed to the astounded, delighted, almost disbelieving pair tied to the dais steps that the remaining alien tried to run in at least three directions at one and the same time. But then, before the lone survivor of the unknown vengeance from the night sky could even cry out, as finally he made to bolt from the cobbled square, down swooped a great, black-faced bat-shape that struck him from his feet and was upon him, knife glinting redly, all in one fluid motion. A second later, it was all over. De Marigny had acted with a murderous efficiency born of utter horror and loathing. He felt not the slightest repugnance at the fact that he had so ruthlessly destroyed these three abominations of darkest dream.

Without pause the avenging dreamer leapt to the steps of the dais, where it was the work of seconds to cut the captives loose. All this time Titus Crow had spoken not a word. His mouth hung half open in amazement and his eyes were wide in disbelief. Finally, as de Marigny helped the two to their feet, averting his eyes as best he could from Tiania's nakedness, Crow blurted: 'Henri! De Marigny! It's you under that blacking! But how? You, here in dreamland? God! But I've never been more –'

'Later, Titus,' de Marigny cut him off. 'Heaven knows we've little enough time right now. I'll take Tiania first – the cloak can't manage three – but I'll be back for you immediately. Better grab yourself one of those scimitars in case more of these beasts come on the scene. I'll be as quick as I can.' With that he turned to Tiania, who in turn looked to Crow for guidance.

'Trust de Marigny, Tiania,' the bruised and bloodied man told her. 'He is the greatest friend a man ever had.' He gave the girl into his friend's care, and the latter, more than ever aware of Tiania's nakedness and unearthly beauty, wrapped her quickly in a wing of his cloak. Without further pause he took firm hold of her and flew up into darkness. They sped quickly to a tall unlighted tower about a mile from the dais of the ruby, and there de Marigny quietly deposited Tiania behind the balcony of the flat roof. Before he could fly off again she caught him by the arm.

'Titus has told me much of you, Henri-Laurent de Marigny,' she whispered. 'I understand now why he left me alone in Elysia to return to your green Earth. Friends such as you are singularly rare. He loves you as a brother, and from this time on so do I.'

She leaned forward and kissed de Marigny lightly upon his mouth. A moment later, as he soared off again into the night, his heart also soared within him. And de Marigny knew that come what may he had already been rewarded fully for whatever risks he was taking here in Earth's dreamland.

A minute or so later de Marigny picked up Titus Crow

from the square of the ruby dais, and then it became obvious to him just how much the latter's ordeals had taken out of him; scimitar grasped in one hand, Crow was barely capable of hanging on as they flew up into the night. De Marigny asked his strangely fatigued friend how long he and Tiania had languished upon the steps of the dais.

'Since noon, Henri, but we were weak enough before ever we got to Dylath-Leen. They brought us to the city in one of their vile black galleys, and never a bite to eat in three days. I was drugged and only half-conscious all of that time, but even wide awake I could never have eaten the unnameable slop they offered us! And don't forget that we've been tied beneath that monstrous abnormality in the square for nigh on eleven hours. That alone has robbed me of more energy than the three days spent in that galley rolled into one.

'Tiania is amazing. There's more of the Elder Gods in her than you'd ever guess – even taking into account her unearthly beauty – and I fancy that's what saved her from being greatly affected by proximity to the great ruby. As for me, all I need is a bite of plain, decent food, a little rest, and I'll soon be my normal self again. Or my *ab*normal self, if you will. I don't suppose you brought a bottle of brandy with you, Henri? By God, that would cheer me up no end!'

In spite of all his worries, de Marigny had to grin. This was typical of the Titus Crow he knew, a far cry from the forlorn and desperate figure so recently tied fast to the steps of the ruby dais. Indeed, Crow had not been understating that vast jewel's debilitating influence, and as the distance between the flyers and the ruby increased, so something of Crow's former strength and zest began to return. De Marigny knew that when that strength had returned fully, then indeed would Titus Crow be a force to reckon with, and it would certainly be a dark hour for the evil influences at present operating in Earth's dreamland.

And de Marigny understood what his friend had meant by referring to himself as being 'abnormal.' During his adventures in space and time, on his way to Elysia, Crow had crashed the time-clock into an alien world. Rescued from oblivion by a robot doctor, T3RE, Crow had been rebuilt from the pulp of his human body by a science beyond anything even guessed at by the doctors and scientists of his mother world. He was immensely strong and fast; he could stay underwater without mechanical aids for indefinite periods; his skin was impervious to all but the most corrosive atmospheres; and, perhaps most amazing of all, he had been built in the image of himself as he had been twenty to twenty-five years earlier! Even Crow's mind had been altered! He had found himself able to do completely inexplicable and unbelievable things with the time-clock, using it in ways never conceived of by its original builders, the Elder Gods themselves.

De Marigny banished all such thoughts and memories from his mind as he caused the cloak to drop them down to the roof of the tower. With a little cry of relief Tiania threw herself into Crow's arms. He stroked her for a moment, then turned to their rescuer:

'Well, Henri, what do you have in mind now? We're not out of the fire yet, my friend.'

'I know that, but –' de Marigny began, then paused and put a finger to his lips as suddenly sounds of activity began to drift up from the nighted city. Below, some distance away, freshly lighted torches flared redly. The man in the flying cloak turned a wide-eyed look to his companions. 'That sounds like trouble. It looks like they've discovered your escape!'

Night-Gaunt

'They'll soon alert the whole city,' de Marigny continued in haste as he tried to rearrange his plans. 'Titus, how many of them are there in Dylath-Leen?'

'A thousand, possibly more,' Crow answered. 'We saw a regular fleet of their black galleys in the harbor.'

'Then we've no time to lose. Same as last time, I'll take Tiania first and see if I can get her to a safe place beyond the watchfires at the perimeter of the city. Then I'll be back for you. Lie low, Titus, until I get back.'

Crow clapped his friend on the back and wished him luck, then squatted down behind the tower's parapet wall. A second later de Marigny was once again airborne, with Tiania wrapped in a wing of his cloak. As they flew on high, looking down at the squares and rooftops of nighted Dylath-Leen, they could see that indeed the horned horrors from Leng were beginning to throng the city's streets.

With the fingers of his free hand upon the studs that controlled the cloak's antigravitic forces, and his other arm wrapped firmly around Tiania's tiny waist, de Marigny coaxed the clock up higher still into the night air. The girl clung tightly to him, but though the swiftflowing air was chill, their height above the ground fearful, and the tension increasing with each passing moment, not once did she tremble.

He believed she must be thinking about Titus Crow, left behind now atop the tower in the middle of an unquiet city, and to divert her mind from any morbid train of thought, he said: 'You're a brave girl, Tiania.'

She immediately turned her head toward him and smiled through the rush of dark air, and de Marigny believed he could see the worry and fear swiftly fading from her lovely, almost luminous face. 'I'm not really brave,' she said. 'In the care of two such as you and Titus, what can there be to fear?'

It was de Marigny's turn to smile; but a second later he frowned, asking: 'Why in the name of all that's wonderful didn't you two bring flying cloaks with you to dreamland? I should have thought that –'

'But we did bring cloaks,' she cut him off, 'and would have brought a time-clock, too, except that it would give the game away. Our cloaks were taken from us by those horned beasts when they trapped us. The fools, they threw them away with the rest of our clothes!'

'They didn't know what they were?'

'No. Creatures such as they are could never dream of flying. Their very souls are earthbound.'

'And how were you trapped in the first place?' de Marigny asked, noting that the watchfires were slowly falling away to the rear. He stared ahead into darkness, hoping to find a good place to alight.

'That is a long story, but I will try to be brief . . .

'When first we came here there were many things we should have done. We ought first to have visited Atal the Wise, and perhaps Kuranes of Ooth-Nargai beyond the Tanarian Hills. But there seemed so many wonders to see – almost as many as one might find in Elysia – and it was the first time I had ever been in an alien world, even a dream world. Also, I wanted Titus for myself for a little while. And so I persuaded him to spend just a day or two in idle wandering from town to town, spending the nights at tiny inns and taverns. To me it was just a game, you see. I did not know . . .

'Anyway, Titus agreed to my silly ideas, saying it would be a good way to acclimatize ourselves, to get the feel of dreamland. We used our cloaks very discreetly, usually traveling in the hours immediately before dawn. Thus, distance was no problem.

'Those first two days were wonderful; then in Ath –

'Ath is an unpleasant little place bordering on Istharta. Neither Titus nor I liked it much and we did not stay there long. But while we were there Titus was given a lead to follow. It was a false lead, but we did not know that then. We were told by a man of dreamland – a traitor, in league with the dark forces of nightmare, a dupe of powers unnatural in dream who must have somehow known who we were and why we were here – that we should go to the Isle of Oriab, across the Southern Sea. He told us to go to Baharna, the great seaport, where we would find a black galley whose captain would be able to tell us all we needed to know of the troubles besetting dreamland, perhaps even how to deal with those troubles.

'We went to Baharna, arriving late in the evening when the wharves were all in darkness. The captain of the black galley, a squat little man who kept himself in the shadows, told us to go to a certain tavern, that he would meet us there upon the morrow. The tavern was a wharfside place, none too clean and somehow depressing, where furtive figures seemed to hide in dark corners. But our room was the best in the house, and the food and wine seemed excellent . . . The food, the wine too – they were drugged! We woke up captives of the black galley, and . . . but the rest you know.'

De Marigny nodded. 'Well, it's all over now. And look there!' he pointed sharply down into the darkness. 'That's it, that white rock there. It's not too high or steep for you to climb down from should . . . should anything happen. And it's a landmark I can't miss when I return with Titus. Down we go, Tiania.'

He caused the cloak to drop them gently down to a wide ledge halfway up the peak that jutted stark and white from the desert's sands. There he deposited Tiania, telling her that it would not be long before he brought Titus to her, and then that they would all three be in Ulthar in time for breakfast. It was not to be so, but de Marigny could not know that.

To Titus Crow, waiting behind the parapet wall of the tower only a mile from the unquiet center of Dylath-Leen, it seemed an inordinately long time indeed before de Marigny came silently winging down once more out of the night to alight beside him like some great bat. 'Henri,' Crow whispered, 'is all well?'

The low hush of his voice was not unwarranted. The streets below were alive with torch-bearing search parties, so that Dylath-Leen was a maze of redly flickering flames and leaping shadows – and now from all directions could be heard the hideous, ululant alert-cries of the horned ones from nighted Leng. Indeed the sound of hurrying footsteps even echoed up to them from the street directly beneath their tall refuge.

'So far so good,' de Marigny breathlessly answered. 'Tiania is safe for the moment. I think we're just about in the clear, Titus. This flying cloak of yours must take all the credit, though. Without it I could have done nothing.'

'The cloak is yours now, Henri – you've earned it. Here, tuck this sword into your belt. Now, just let me get a firm grip. Right, up we go!'

More slowly this time, feeling the burden of Titus Crow's greater weight, the flying cloak lifted the two friends into the night air over Dylath-Leen, and both men were greatly relieved when the flickering torchfires had dimmed and fallen away below and behind them. It was not long then before other fires sprang up in red relief to their front, and soon after that they were flying high above the watchfires at the rim of the city.

'A mile, perhaps two miles more,' said de Marigny.

'There's a jagged fang of white rock sticking up out of the desert. That's where I left Tiania. We'll be there in another minute or so.'

'And what then, Henri – a series of short hops to Ulthar?'

'Something like that, I think, yes.'

'Good. And as soon as we've rested up a little and found safe lodging for Tiania, then we're off to Ilek-Vad. I want to know just exactly what's going on there. Yes, and you might even find time to tell me what the devil you're doing here in Earth's dreamland, when by all rights you should be well on your way to Elysia.'

'I *am* on my way to Elysia, Titus. This is the only way I'm ever likely to get there. Kthanid asked me to come, telling me that you and Tiania were in trouble. I'll tell you the whole story later. As for Ilek-Vad: yes, I, too, would like to know what's going on there. After all, that's where my father is. I don't remember a great deal about him, but –'

'There's your white rock dead ahead!' Crow suddenly cried, cutting his friend off short. He pointed eagerly. 'And there's Tiania, I can see her waving. Oh, well done, Henri. You're not an inch off course!'

Controlling the cloak's descent, de Marigny brought them drifting down toward the ledge where the girl-goddess waited. She waved again, reaching out her arms to them as they approached out of the darkness.

It was only then – as the two men felt a rushing blast of air, a buffeting gust much stronger and quite different from any normal draught they might expect to meet during their steady flight above the desert – that they realized something was greatly amiss. The freakish, turbulent eddy tossed them to one side, so that they crashed shoulders-on into the sheer wall of the rock at a point some thirty feet to one side of Tiania. Here the drop was sheer to the desert's floor, and de Marigny had to manipulate the cloak's studs to draw back from the white rock's jagged face. As he did so he heard Crow's sharp intake of breath, and following his friend's horrified gaze he saw and recognized a huge gray shape that passed noiselessly by, circling the rocky spire on membrane wings.

'Night-gaunt!' cried de Marigny, fighting to regain control of the cloak as it was caught again in the wash of the creature's wings. 'A great gray gaunt!'

'Put me down on that ledge, quick!' Crow shouted. 'That damn thing must be after Tiania! Look – here it comes again!'

For the third time they felt the turbulence of the huge night-gaunt's wings as they flapped in leathery sentience, suspending their rubbery owner directly over the girl who now crouched terrified on the ledge of the white rock. Now they were able to get a reasonably clear view of the thing, better by far than de Marigny's previous look at such creatures received through Kthanid's telepathic knowledge-imparting.

The horror, while being twice as big as any of its loathsome species viewed before, was nevertheless endowed with the same noxiously thin outline as lesser gaunts and wore precisely the same aspect. Horns sprouted from its faceless head; it was barb-tailed and bat-winged; its skin looked rubbery, cold, and damp – and, possibly worst of all, it was utterly silent.

Then de Marigny was rushed abruptly aloft as Crow let go his hold on the cloak's harness to leap to the ledge close to Tiania. Yet again struggling to bring the cloak under his control, de Marigny all but missed what followed next. As it was he heard Crow's cry of rage and horror . . . and he saw the gray shape of that giant among night-gaunts as it lifted skyward on silently beating pinions, bearing aloft the wriggling, shrieking, slender form of Tiania grasped in prehensile paws!

4

Atal's Elixir

On the wide ledge of the white rock's peak high above the desert, Titus Crow raged silently in the night and shook his scimitar at the diminishing gray shape that flapped away against a background of strange constellations. By the time de Marigny had landed beside him, however, the naked giant had recovered his equilibrium sufficiently to cry out in a half-choked voice: 'Quickly, man, out of the cloak! Hurry, Henri, I must get after that monster!'

Seeing instantly how useless and time-consuming it would be to argue – aware that the cloak was designed to operate at maximum efficiency with only one passenger and that it was Titus Crow's prerogative to pursue the huge night-gaunt and rescue Tiania, if such was at all possible – de Marigny immediately unfastened the cloak's harness and helped Crow into it. Then, without another word spoken, Crow grabbed his friend around the waist with one arm, his other hand flying to the collar studs that controlled the cloak. Another moment saw de Marigny deposited none too gently on the desert's sandy floor.

Rising again into the night, Crow called: 'Can you find your way back to Ulthar, Henri?'

'I know the way,' de Marigny shouted back. 'Five miles or so from here I pick up the Skai and simply follow the river. No need to worry about me, Titus. I'll see you in Ulthar . . . both of you! Good luck!'

'Thanks. I fancy I'll need all the luck I can get,' Crow's answer came back from the heights. 'Take care, Henri.' For a moment or two he was a vague batshape against the blue crystal stars, then he was gone.

Half an hour and a little more than two miles later, as he strode out over the desert dunes in the direction of Ulthar, led on by the sweet scent of night-blooming flowers on the banks of the Skai, de Marigny glanced for the tenth time apprehensively over his shoulder. It was his imagination, of course, but for the last twenty minutes or so, since shortly after he set out from the foot of the white rock pinnacle, he had had the feeling that he was being followed. Yet each time he looked back there was nothing to be seen, only the low dunes and occasionally the rock jutting starkly against the night-dark sky.

Climbing to the top of a high dune, he glanced back yet again and this time spied in the distance the darkly looming basalt towers of Dylath-Leen. No healthy lights showed in the city, only a dull glow from the watchfires at its rim. It shocked de Marigny to be reminded how close he still was to that nightmare-cursed city, and he determined there and then to increase his distance from it as rapidly as humanly possible. It did not seem likely that the horned ones could be on his trail already, and yet –

He shuddered and felt the short hairs rise at the back of his neck, a reaction not alone engendered of the desert's chill, and turned once more toward friendly Ulthar; but even as he turned he saw a movement in the corner of his eye. Something had slipped silently from shadow to shadow less than a hundred yards to his rear. Now he remembered something Grant Enderby had told him – about how expert the horned ones were at tracking their prey – and he shuddered again.

Quickly de Marigny slid down the side of the dune and looked about for a vantage point. He ran for a boulder that lay half-buried in the sand and hid behind it. As he went to his knees in the shadows he heard a distant but distinct wail rising in the night air. The cry reached its highest note, quavered inquiringly, then died into eerie silence. It was almost immediately answered by a second call, from a point de Marigny judged to be just beyond the tall dune; and while these were not the ululant alert cries with which he was now familiar, nevertheless the dreamer knew that they were given voice by those same horned horrors from Leng!

Now de Marigny shot frantic glances to left and right, his eyes searching the desert's starlit gloom for areas of deeper shadow that might hide his onward flight toward the river. And as he did so there came to his ears many more of the inquiring cries – except that now certain of the creatures who uttered those hideous bayings obviously flanked him! Indeed, one of those cries had seemed to come from somewhere *behind* where he crouched, from the direction of the Skai itself. And this cry had been different in that it had seemed somehow – triumphant?

So intent was he upon gauging the exact directions whence these latter sounds had issued that he almost failed to hear the soft footfalls in the sand. Too late, he did hear them, and he turned with a single gasp of horror in time to see only the jeweled hilt of a scimitar in the instant before it struck him between the eyes . . .

When de Marigny regained consciousness he believed for a moment that he had somehow returned through the barriers of dream to the waking world. But not so. Though the sun stood at its zenith and hurt his eyes behind his fluttering eyelids, the dreamer knew that indeed he was still a prisoner of dreamland; more than ever a prisoner, for the buildings and towers that loomed blackly upwards before him, and the steps that sent knives of pain lancing into his spine where he was tied to them were a basalt quarried in dreamland. This could only be Dylath-Leen; and sure enough, if he tilted his head right back at an angle he could see – the great ruby!

'Ah, our friend from the waking world of men has finally

returned to us – with a very sick head, no doubt!' The squat speaker leaned carelessly on the hilt of his scimitar, its point digging into the rough grain of the steps and its blade curving uncomfortably close to de Marigny's rib cage. The coarse black silk of the horned one's baggy breeches was stained and grimed, the red sash at his waist festooned with knives. He wore huge rubies in the rings on his fat fingers and an evil grin upon his face, in which veiled, slightly slanted eyes regarded de Marigny almost hungrily.

And suddenly the dreamer was aware of his pain. His skin felt completely dehydrated, baked dry under the noon sun; his back, which through long hours of unconsciousness had lain across the sharp corners of three of the dais steps, felt as though it might break in pieces at any moment; his head ached abominably and felt grotesquely swollen. Naked, his entire body was bruised from being brutally dragged across miles of desert sands; his lips, tongue, and throat were parched, and leather thongs cut into his wrists and ankles where they were tied.

'Dreamer, we are going to kill you!' This time the speaker emphasized his words by idly kicking de Marigny's bruised ribs. De Marigny barely held back the cry of agony that sprang to his lips, managing at the same time to lift his head up high enough to see that he was ringed by perhaps twenty of the horned ones. Their leader, the speaker, wore no shoes, and de Marigny knew that the extreme pain he had felt when his tender ribs were kicked was due to the fact that his torturer had hooves instead of feet.

'We are going to kill you,' that monstrous being said again, 'but it is entirely up to you how we do it. You can die slowly, very slowly, losing first your hands, then your feet, and your so-called manhood. Then your ears, your eyes, your tongue at the very end. It would take at least a day, perhaps two. *Or you could die the hard way!'*

He paused to let that last sink in, then continued: 'On the other hand, we could be merciful.'

'I doubt,' de Marigny groaned, 'if your sort know the meaning of mercy.'

'Ah, but we do! For instance, it would be merciful to lop off your head with a single stroke – but before you are granted that boon, there are several things I want to know.'

The horned one waited expectantly but de Marigny made no answer.

'If I have your eyes propped open with slivers of wood, and your head tied back, you would very quickly, very painfully go blind. The sun is singularly unkind to those who stare so at her. But before that becomes necessary –'

'– You want to know something.'

'Correct! You have been listening to me. That is good. There are several things I wish to know, yes. One: how did you come into Dylath-Leen so secretively, and manage to kill three of our colleagues so efficiently before they could even raise the alarm? Two: how were you able to smuggle your friends so cleverly, so swiftly away, when you yourself were later caught? Three: where are your friends now, for we must bring them back here in order that they may keep an important appointment. And finally, four: what is in this vial, which was all you carried other than your knife and a length of rope?'

The elixir! De Marigny gasped involuntarily as his questioner mentioned Atal's elixir. He had forgotten about the vial until now. The horned one heard the dreamer's gasp and was quick to note how his eyes had widened fractionally, however momentarily. 'Eh?' he grunted. 'Something I said? About this strange little bottle of liquid, perhaps?' He held the vial out, between thumb and forefinger, where de Marigny could see it.

'A man, with no food, no water, coming out of nowhere

with nothing but a knife, a rope, and this – and yet you somehow succeeded in rescuing your two friends. Amazing! And such a little thing, this vial, to sustain the three of you across the desert to Ulthar. What does it contain?'

De Marigny's brain whirled as he sought an advantageous way to answer the horned one's question. 'A . . . a *poison*,' he finally offered. 'It contains a deadly poison.'

His questioner lifted his scimitar, allowing its point to scrape slowly up the line of de Marigny's ribs, and peered intently at its shiny blade. For a long moment he was silent, then: 'Oh, no, no, no, my friend.' His voice was low now, oily, deadly; his eyes glittered dangerously. 'That will never do. A little vial of poison – no more than a dozen or so drops – to murder an entire city?'

De Marigny writhed both physically and mentally, like a great intelligent moth pinned to some entomologist's card. He had hoped that his interrogator would make him drink his own 'poison' – which by now should have properly fermented – but the ruse had not worked. Then, like a flash of lightning illuminating the dark clouds of the dreamer's mind, there came a scene remembered from his youth. From a book, perhaps, or a cartoon viewed in some moviehouse of childhood. It was the picture of a rabbit: Br'er Rabbit! And suddenly de Marigny believed that there might after all be a way out. He could but try.

'If I tell you what is in the vial – if I reveal the secret of the magical potion it contains – will you swear to set me free unharmed?'

The horned one pretended to give de Marigny's proposal some consideration, fooling the dreamer not at all, then grated: 'Agreed. After all, it is not you we want but the two you stole from us. If what you have to tell us has some bearing on their present whereabouts, then we will set you free.'

Now it was de Marigny's turn to feign deliberation.

Finally he said, 'It is an elixir to increase one's strength tenfold. One sip of the potion – one drop – and a man may leap the tallest dune at one bound, stride over the desert to Ulthar in the space of a single hour, fight like ten men to overcome tremendous odds, aye, and never once feel the effort.'

The horned one folded the vial carefully in his fat fist and stared at de Marigny intently. 'Is this true?'

'How else do you suppose I came out of the night, without provisions, defeating your three guardsmen like so many children to be tossed aside? How else do you explain the utter absence of the two I rescued, gone now like the wind over the desert? Doubtless they are even now in Ulthar, at the Temple of the Elder Ones, where Atal –'

'*Atal!*' hissed his interrogator. 'What do you know of Atal?'

'Why, it was Atal gave me the elixir, to speed me on my quest!'

A murmuring swelled in the crowd of horned ones standing about, mutterings of hatred, of awe and amazement – of greed for the magic elixir, if elixir it was. Now de Marigny's questioner opened his fist once more to stare lustfully at the tiny bottle it contained. Then his expression grew very sly.

'No, I do not believe you. I think that after all it is perhaps a poison, and that you would trick me into tasting it. If so, then –' He quickly unstoppered the vial and thrust it toward de Marigny's face. The dreamer, expecting that this might happen, lifted up his head and opened his mouth wide, straining his neck to reach the tiny bottle.

Immediately the horned one snatched back his arm. He grinned evilly. 'So your story *is* true! It . . . must be.' His grin was quickly replaced by a look of strange anticipation. He licked his wide lips and his hand actually trembled as once more he studied the vial with wide eyes.

'Let me try it, Garl,' came a guttural rasp from one who stood behind the leader.

'No, me,' another voice demanded.

'Hold!' Garl held up his hand. 'There is still one question unanswered.' He turned his gaze once more to de Marigny's face. 'If indeed you tell the truth, how was it we caught you so easily? Why did you not escape, like your friends, by leaping away over the dunes and speeding to Ulthar?'

'Simple.' De Marigny attempted a shrug as best he could. 'I neglected to heed Atal's warning.'

'Which was?'

'Too much of the elixir affects a man like too much wine, slowing him down and dulling his senses for a while. After freeing the other two dreamers, thinking to make myself stronger and faster still, I took a second sip of the elixir. Before I knew it –'

'We caught you. Hmm! I believe you, yes. And I also believe that with the aid of your elixir we might even recapture the ones you freed. But first the elixir's powers must be tested.'

'I'll test it, Garl,' came a concerted babble of cries from the crowding horned ones.

'Me!'

'No, let me be the one, Garl!'

De Marigny's inquisitor turned on his colleagues. 'What? You'd all like to be stronger than Garl, would you?' He laughed and shook a fat finger at them. 'None of that, my lads. The elixir is far too precious to waste on fools and hotheads. Later, perhaps, I'll handpick a raiding party – and tonight we'll look for certain absent friends in Ulthar – but right now I myself will test the illustrious Atal's elixir! Stand back, all of you!'

Though the sun blazed high overhead, it was not the heat of that golden orb that brought fresh streams of sweat to de Marigny's brow but the slow and deliberate way in which Garl of Leng lifted one hand up to his alien face – that and the way his other hand lifted high his scimitar.

'If you have lied to me, dreamer, then at least you'll have earned yourself a quick death. That is the only bonus such lies will bring you, however. And now –' He barely touched his lips to the rim of the tilted vial.

First a look of puzzlement changed the horned one's features, then a frown. 'A not unpleasant taste,' he began, 'though somewhat –' Then he reeled drunkenly backward down the dais steps, his scimitar falling with a clatter from a suddenly spastic hand that clawed its way to his throat. He swayed at the foot of the dais for a second only, bulging eyes fixed upon the vial still clenched in one shaking hand.

Then his outline wavered; he seemed to puff outwards as his flesh became a mist; finally his clothes fell in a silken rain to the cobbles of the square. The vial fell too, cushioned by the coarse silks. Hanging in the air, all that remained of Garl was a rapidly diminishing echo, a thin squeal of outrage and horror!

Then de Marigny's hoarse laughter broke the stunned silence. Hearing the derision in the dreamer's voice, the awed crowd of horned ones was galvanized into activity. As one of them stooped to snatch up the fallen vial and others fought over the remaining silks, the rest ringed de Marigny on the steps. Scimitars whispered from scabbards and flashed in the sun, and for a moment the dreamer thought that he was done for. Then –

'Hold, lads!' shouted the one who had snatched up the vial. 'I, Barzt, now lead you – and I claim the right to avenge Garl myself. But first there is something I must know.' He tickled de Marigny's throat with the point of his scimitar. 'You, man from the waking world, dreamer. Where have you sent Garl with your dark magic?'

'He's gone to a hell worse than anything even you could imagine,' de Marigny chuckled. 'Worse by far than any torture you could apply to me. You see, the "elixir" was a poison after all, the key to a gate which opens to the blackest hells. Even now Garl screams in eternal agony, where he will curse me in his torment forever; but I am safe from him here in dreamland. Kill me now, if you will, for I am satisfied that Garl has paid for the deaths of my two friends from the waking world. They, too, drank of the poison rather than suffer the indignities of your vile paws. Kill me – kill me now!' He offered up his throat. 'Only –'

De Marigny paused, as if biting his tongue, feigning sudden horror. Then, to the crowding horned ones, it seemed as if he attempted to cringe into himself upon the dais steps. 'No!' he forced a strangled cry from parched lips. 'No, not . . . not *that!*'

'Wha –?' began the frowning Barzt. Then he noticed how de Marigny's terrified eyes had fastened upon the vial he held so gingerly away from his vile body. And Barzt's eyes lit at once with a fiendish delight.

'So!' he cried. 'Garl will curse you in his torment forever, will he? Well then, go to this hell you speak so eloquently of, dreamer, where you, too, may suffer its eternal torments – *and* Garl's tender mercies!' So saying, standing on the dreamer's hair to hold his head still, he stooped and touched the vial to de Marigny's lips.

But no sooner was the oddly shaped bottle at his lips than he licked its moist rim with a darting tongue. Barzt sensed that he had been fooled, but it was too late. In the space of another second or so de Marigny seemed to fill out like a limp balloon suddenly inflated with air, and even as his form wavered and disappeared the horned ones noted the look of glad triumph that lit in his eyes.

And in the wake of his vanishing they heard the echoes of joyous laughter.

Part Four

1

Beyond the Peaks of Throk

Subduing his raging fury as best he could, yet totally incapable of curbing the sick feeling of horror that lay thick in his stomach like bile – horror for Tiania in the clutches of that flying beast-thing that soared somewhere ahead in the darkness over the desert – Titus Crow leaned into the wind and rode his cloak like a great bat through the night. He followed the occasional shriek from Tiania, dread draining him every time he heard her cry out, until at last he realized that she was deliberately screaming, creating a trail by means of which he could follow the flightpath of the great night-gaunt.

And it dawned on him too that, plucky girl though she was, she might save some of her breath for later – when perhaps they might both have more need of screaming. Indeed, the flight of the night-gaunt seemed arrow-straight, and Crow's instinct told him where the beast was headed. Then, as its outline momentarily obliterated a great whorl of stars hanging low in the sky ahead, he caught a glimpse of the thing and knew he had been correct. Unlike its cousins, the common gaunts, by virtue of its gigantic size, nevertheless this faceless terror of the night made for a region of dreamland where Titus Crow knew that the lesser gaunts proliferated. He put on a burst of speed to shorten, if possible, the monster's lead.

Out over the Southern Sea sped the great gaunt, and far below Tiania could see all the stars of the night sky reflected in black mirror waters. Normally she would have found such a sight beautiful indeed, but now, dangling from the rubbery paws of this clammy creature as it soared silently through the upper air of dreamland, she shuddered and cried out yet again. She knew that Titus Crow must be somewhere behind the great night-gaunt, knew too that her cries must eventually guide him to her; for while the gaunt could not fly on forever, Crow's cloak was utterly tireless.

Behind her now, Tiania could make out the dim lights of small towns spread along the coast of the Southern Sea, and briefly from far below there came drifting the song of a lone fisherman at the helm of his night-becalmed vessel. Doubtless he was singing to ward off the dark spirits of the night waters, which legend had it walked on the glassy surface of the deep when the nights were calm.

Then, far to the east, Tiania saw the first thin gray line of light curving on the distant horizon. True dawn was still hours away, but the promise of a new day was already aborning. She wondered what the new day would bring, and she thought with longing of faerie Elysia, many dimensions away in space and time. Love of Elysia was strong in Tiania, but love of Titus Crow was stronger. Though she was no longer afraid, she cried out yet again in the darkness, praying that her voice would ride back to her Earthman on the night wind. He would not answer, dared not alert the monstrous creature that carried her high above the Southern Sea of his presence, but as certain to Tiania as the beating of her own pure heart was the knowledge that he was there.

Thus the hours sped by, until chilled and weary, utterly depleted by her adventures, the girl-goddess fell asleep in the grip of the great gaunt. And perhaps fate smiled at Tiania in her innocence, for a warm wind from far exotic lands found her there where she lay between the night-gaunt's clammy paws, lulling her into dreams within dreams which were not at all nightmarish.

Titus Crow, too, saw the thin gray light on the horizon,

and he urged still more speed from his cloak and streamlined himself to cleave the air more cleanly. He believed that with the dawn the huge night-gaunt would find a cave or crevice in which to sleep and while away the hours of daylight, like less fabulous nocturnal beasts of the waking world. And he wanted to be in view of the creature when it went to ground.

For some time now he had listened intently for Tiania's cries coming back to him on the wind, but in vain, and while he was fairly certain of the direction in which the great gaunt headed, nevertheless he would dearly love to hear the girl's golden voice confirming his guess. Then, as dawn turned the horizon into a gray mist, he spied the vapor-wreathed Isle of Oriab ahead, and against the pale of dawn a nightmare shape that fell down and down toward far Ngranek.

Crow's spirits immediately revived. He had been right, then. The great gaunt's destination was indeed Ngranek, haunt of all the lesser gaunts of night. Now he flew more carefully, keeping his presence secret, for he was closer to the monster than he had dared hope. Down toward Ngranek's peak spiraled the gaunt, with Titus Crow behind it, down toward the mouths of certain caves that opened to the cavernously honeycombed interior of that mountain.

Now Crow could see the strange face cut in vast outlines on that side of the peak forever hidden to Oriab's peoples, the face carved more in the likeness of a strange god than a man. And looking down from on high he saw far beneath those carven features the sterile lava abysses which marked the wrath of the Great Gods of Eld . . . even here in Earth's dreamland! Now, seeing for himself this proof positive of a mighty battle long forgotten and beyond the meager imagination of men, he knew indeed that Ngranek was a peak ancient beyond words.

But Titus Crow had little enough time to study these

things or ponder their import. He had seen the great gaunt settling on high-arched wings toward a black cave mouth, and now he flew his cloak as swiftly as he could in that direction. Around and about this cavern entrance flew a flock of lesser gaunts in apparently aimless circles, and for all that they were more than twice the size of a man they scattered in terror as Crow hurtled through their midst. Then, after he had passed by, they hung in the brightening dawn air in sleepy, faceless bewilderment. And down, down into Ngranek's inner darkness went Titus Crow, flying blind now and of necessity more slowly, following only the muffled throb of vast and leathery wings.

It seemed to the cloaked dreamer that he flitted down through inconceivable gulfs of night; but then, as his eyes grew more accustomed to the gloom, he saw that the dark air was semiluminous with a gray phosphorescence. Moments later he descended into reeking clouds of mist that may well have had their origin in Earth's core.

And now, high above, a monstrously vast ceiling of stalactites stretched away into dim distances, while below marched the ominous needles of spires which could only be the fabulous Peaks of Throk. Down and down, ever deeper the cloak carried Crow into this underworld of dream, until the stark gray Peaks of Throk reached up immense and ageless on all sides. And then the needle tips of those peaks were lost in legendary heights and their feet in darkest depths, so that it seemed to the dreamer he fell between numberless pillars going down to infinity. And always he followed the throb of tremendous, rubbery wings.

Then, for what seemed an interminable time, there came buffeting, howling winds that blew Crow far off course; and struggle as he might against this unexpected maelstrom of air, he could do nothing but pray that he would not be hurled against the granite pillars that loomed on all sides. Now, too, he found his view obscured by clouds of sulphurous ash and smoke; but at last the winds calmed down, the smoke cleared, and far away the dreamer saw the Peaks of Throk receding into flickering, pale-blue death-fires. Then there was only darkness and a distant, weary-sounding throbbing of monstrous wings.

Knowing that by now he could only be in the fabled Vale of Pnoth, where the enormous dholes dig their burrows and pile their cairns of bones, Crow felt something of the unreasoning terror that all dreamers know in the face of nightmare. For this was that place where all the ghouls of the waking world are reputed to throw the remains of their graveyard feasts. Titus Crow desired to meet neither ghouls nor dholes, and so he put on a burst of speed in the direction of the now fading throbbing.

Again he was flying blind, in near-solid darkness, but his instinct did not desert him; and as he rushed through reeking ebony vaults he reminded himself over and over again that many things are far simpler in dream. But then he uttered a short, harsh sardonic bark of self-derision as he wondered why, if this were really so, he was finding things so difficult!

Beneath him now as he flew he could hear a dry rustling, which he guessed must be the sound that dholes make in their singular bone-heaping occupations; and once he brushed against something that loomed up vast and slimy in his path. Then ahead he saw a bright point of light that soon grew into a painful white glare. Approaching the source of this harsh illumination, he saw that it was a natural cave that led back into the face of a sheer wall of granite. A moment later a great gray shadow flitted eerily and silently along the path of white light to disappear into the cave beyond.

Titus Crow's mechanical heart seemed to give a great leap within him then, for at the last he had seen a limp, slender form hanging from that shadow's tiredly drooping paws! Now, reassuring himself, he fondled the hilt of his scimitar where it hung from the belt of his cloak's harness, and he allowed himself a low grunt of grim anticipation as he drove for the bright cave's entrance.

It was then, as he entered into a tremendously vast white cavern, that the disaster occurred. Fortunately for Titus Crow the thing came immediately after he cleared the cave's entrance, when he was flying only a few feet above the white sands that floored the fantastic cavern. If he had been at a greater height . . . it did not bear thinking about.

For without warning his cloak suddenly disappeared, vanishing utterly and without trace in an instant, leaving him prone in thin air, diving forward in a downward curve that could only end in the white sand! A second later came the shock of impact and momentary oblivion, then painful consciousness. He spat out sand and picked himself up; shaken and awed, he stared all about. The cloak had quite definitely vanished, so useless to worry or wonder about the hows or whys of it – and anyway there were other, more important things to think about.

Staring across the desert of white sand, Crow's eyes narrowed as he picked out a vague movement in the middle distance. Instinct warned him that there were terrible dangers here, for himself as well as the girl-goddess, and if Tiania of Elysia was to be rescued unharmed from this unknown place, then he must face those dangers alone, naked and on foot . . .

2

Perchance to Dream

De Marigny came joyously awake in the time-clock, whirling in orbit high above the Earth. His awakening was instantaneous, without any of the usual transitory dullness of mind and physical sloth, so that he immediately remembered all that had happened. Indeed, his *removal* from dreamland to the waking world was so complete that its effect upon his senses was more a physical than a purely mental thing; for a few moments he felt that his body as well as his mind had been transported. Then the truth of the matter sank in, and as his somewhat shaky laughter terminated in a ringing shout of triumph, he realized that his ploy against the horned ones in Dylath-Leen had been completely successful.

It was only when this initial euphoria began to wear off that de Marigny saw the several rather less than pleasing circumstances of his escape. One: he was wearing the flying cloak, which could only mean that Titus Crow no longer wore it. Then he remembered what Atal had told him about the elixir – how one sip would immediately transport a dreamer back to the waking world, *along with anything he had brought into dreamland with him!* Knowing that in all likelihood Titus Crow depended upon the cloak for his own and Tiania's lives, de Marigny found this last train of thought too unpleasant to follow up. Instead he turned to problem number two: his main reason for wanting to wake up had been to return at once to dreamland, this time taking the time-clock with him. How might he do this now, when he had never felt more fully awake in his entire life?

Now, furious that everything he did seemed to be working out adversely, he cursed himself soundly. Atal's elixir, as far as Henri-Laurent de Marigny was concerned, had performed its function marvelously – but its effect now was that of a strong stimulant, and there seemed no guarantee at all that this effect would soon wear off. He cursed himself again. Of course, it could hardly have been foreseen, but it would have been so simple to ask Atal for something, some drug or 'potion' with which he might return himself to dreamland.

Then de Marigny's eyes lit with inspiration and he snapped his fingers. A drug to return him to dreamland? Why, he knew of something that could do the job admirably. Alcohol!

He was not a great drinker, but he did enjoy a glass of brandy. A double invariably quickened his mind. Another, taken immediately after the first, usually made him tingle. A third would dull his senses considerably, and a fourth –

Half a bottle should see him back to dreamland almost as quickly as he could drink it! One of his few, hasty, last-minute provisions prior to setting out for Elysia had been to load the time-clock with three bottles of the very best cognac. These had been for Titus Crow, for good brandies were Crow's one weakness. Now he opened one of the bottles and took a long, deep draft, coughing and spluttering as the first 'bite' of the fluid inflamed his throat. Crow, he knew, would have called him a barbarian; but doubtless he would also have agreed that the deadly serious nature of the situation demanded a rapid solution, however drastic.

Halfway through the bottle, de Marigny felt his head begin to spin quite independently of the whirling timeclock (the motion of which, impossibly, he was beginning to believe he could now actually feel) and suddenly he found himself incapable of repressing a short burst of uproarious laughter. Also, a haze was definitely creeping over his brain, but much too slowly. He took another mouthful of the warming, heady fluid, and yet another. Then, as he removed the bottle from his lips, he staggered.

Now, he knew that it was quite impossible for him to physically stagger inside the clock. While Titus Crow could use the machine both as a gateway into all space and time and as a vehicle proper, de Marigny simply was not yet adept enough for that. Indeed, his one effort in that direction had been completely involuntary, almost disastrous. Therefore he recognized the fact, however vaguely, that he had 'staggered' mentally. In short, he knew now that he was very nearly drunk.

By this time only an inch or so of brandy remained in the bottle. De Marigny peered at it curiously for a moment, swilled it about – then yawned. No more than twenty minutes had elapsed since he started on his solitary binge, but he grinned lopsidedly and began to sing, finishing the bottle off between repeated bursts of the following four lines:

> 'Oh, carry me back to dreamland,
> That's the way to go, to go.
> Carry me back to dreamland,
> You space-time so-and-so!'

The minutes passed steadily and de Marigny's singing occasionally faltered, picking up intermittently as he struggled to keep the song going. Finally the bottle slipped from his fingers – but he was not aware of it.

Outside the clock, had there been someone to observe it, it would at that moment seem that the stars themselves blurred, if only for a moment, and that the disc of Earth trembled in its inexorable orbit of the mighty solar furnace. It might seem, for a moment, that the entire scene were viewed through smoke or warm, rising air – and that then, in the next instant, things were once more as they had always been.

But they were not . . .

3

Creatures of the Cave

White crystal sands shifted beneath Titus Crow's naked feet. He stood under a great white roof that formed a sky reflecting the whiteness of the desert. And the floor of the vast cavern surely was a desert. Miles of bleached sand stretched to the limits of vision in dunes and hills, and the only relief in this blinding monotony was a dark dot moving in the middle distance.

The dreamer had no idea where the blinding light of the place came from – that brightness which so garishly illumined every feature of what ought to have been one of the underworld's blackest pits – but in any case he was far more concerned about other things. One of those things, the one uppermost in his mind, was the agitated motion of the distant dot.

He found his scimitar where it had fallen from the belt of his disappearing cloak, then turned to face in the direction of the peculiar movements. He watched the disturbance grow with a startling swiftness. Soon the single moving shape split amoeba-like into two – one up and one down – and in only a few seconds more the two took on definite forms. Spiraling up from the lower form he could see regular white puffs of sand.

The hairs at the back of Titus Crow's neck suddenly stiffened. At first he had thought that the moving object must be that great gaunt which had carried off Tiania; now he could see how wrong he had been. There were in fact three – creatures? One flew, the second rode upon the Flyer's back, the third ran beneath . . . and all three were things of sheerest nightmare!

Of the three as they drew closer, Crow found the tripedal Runner the most fantastic. Though its two outer legs were thin and bent like those of some monstrous spider, nevertheless they were powerfully muscled; they acted as springs or pistons. The inner or center leg was three times as thick as the other two together, straight and horribly hammerlike. The Runner looked like a great freakish three-legged race, with its center leg slamming forward and down, to be hoisted up again and thrust forward by the springy power of its twin companions. The – foot? – at the end of that middle limb was awesome: hugely splayed and webbed, as wide at least as any ten normal feet, clublike. Why! That great foot would crush muscle and bone to pulp as easily and utterly as would a falling northern pine!

Tall though Crow was, the Runner stood at least half as tall again. It had short, stumpy arms – useless appendages to Crow's keen eyes – and a slender neck. But the *face* above that neck! The dreamer shuddered. He had seen similar things in nightmares as a boy: the red, bulging eyes, the dripping fangs in grinning, wide-slit mouths . . .

By now the creatures were much closer and slowing their pace, but still eagerly craning their necks in Crow's direction, obviously appraising him before a concerted attack. The Runner uttered a hideous cry – like the rasp of a file upon an edge of glass, or a giant chalk on a slate – before moving off to one side from beneath the Flyer and its Rider. Crow did not have to turn to follow the creature's movements; the thudding vibrations of the sand under his feet positioned the Runner exactly in his mind's eye. Instead he concentrated upon the other two.

The Flyer was a monstrous, slender worm, with no eyes that Titus Crow could see, just undulant body and gaping beak. Yet, somehow he knew that the thing sensed him keenly and knew of him as he knew of it. The Rider, seated to the rear of the bat-worm's wings, was worse still. A skull-like head set with glaring green eyes surmounted a thin and wiry body, scaled and mottled in squamous shades, with arms of fantastic length hanging like coiled whips at its sides.

Studying these beings of nightmare Crow tightened his grip on his sword. He was aware of their subtle, edging approach. He would have preferred them to come on at their original headlong pace, when he would have relied upon the superb reactions built into his semisynthetic body by the robot T3RE, but they had seemed to sense his tremendous speed and strength and were wary. Indeed, Crow's strength had returned, and now it redoubled as he reconciled himself to battle. It seemed that this was to be the only way he could get on with his pursuit of the great gaunt and Tiania: first, to do battle with these three creatures of the white cavern.

The Flyer and its Rider were still twenty feet or so from the dreamer when he had his first taste of the fight to come. The Rider took first blood when, catching Crow off guard, a razor-clawed tentacle lashed out like the tongue of a chameleon, cutting his cheek. The cut almost touched his eye and caused him to cry out in outrage at the unexpected pain. The tentacle was withdrawn well out of range before he could even bring his scimitar into a defensive position.

Instantly, at sight of the red blood on Crow's cheek, the Rider began to laugh: '*Rhee, rheee, rheee-eee-eee!*' And as the hair of Crow's neck again reacted to this hellish sound, so he sensed the rapid approach of the Runner – from the rear!

Second blood, with a lightning stroke of the scimitar, went to the embattled dreamer. For having perceived the Runner's cowardly rear attack through the shuddering of the sand underfoot, Titus Crow turned and made a headlong dive to one side. And as the Runner pounded by mere inches away, so the scimitar leaped up in Crow's hand to sever at the knee the creature's right outer leg.

The rest of the fight was chaos and nightmare combined. All three of the hideous guardians of the cavern were screaming, particularly the pain-crazed, crippled Runner. The latter was now slewing mindlessly about on its own axis in a welter of gray ichor and white sand. Half blinded by his own blood and that of the Runner, Crow flailed about with his sword, knowing from the deafening cries of the Flyer and its razor-tentacled rider that they were near at hand. He felt his sword arm suddenly caught in a tentacular grip and wrenched at an odd angle, felt the scimitar fly from fingers part-numbed as his forearm almost broke. And then he took his strong square teeth savagely to work on the slimy tentacle coiled crushingly round his arm.

With his free arm he protected his head, all the time working at the tentacle with his teeth and feeling upon his shoulders and back the agony of ripping cuts from the Rider's second vicious appendage. But suddenly, as his mouth filled with a vile fluid from the rubbery limb, he felt himself jerked off his feet and dashed down in the sand. The movement had been convulsive and he guessed that his teeth had found a ticklish nerve. But he had lost his sword.

Free now, he rolled automatically – feeling the burning sting of sand in his torn back, groping for his sword, not knowing where or even in which direction it lay – until his hand came into contact with something solid. He clenched his fingers about the unknown object and rolled onto his back.

There, immediately above him, lancing down, came the vicious beak of the blind Flyer. Just how the awesome bat-worm knew his exact position he could never have guessed, and he had no time for guessing. He jerked up the object grasped in his hand and thrust it between himself and the descending beak. He saw then that his shield was nothing less than the shorn leg of the Runner, which the Flyer at once tore from his grasp and tossed to one side.

Yet, even as Crow gave up his gristly shield he came to his feet, swinging one fist in a deadly arc to smack shatteringly against the side of the lunging beak. The 'bones' of Crow's arms and hands were shaped mainly of an incredibly tough plastic, but the bat-worm's beak, however effective as a weapon, was only of shell-like bone. That great beak cracked open like a hammered egg, and marrow and yellow juices slopped out to further drench the bloodied dreamer.

The Flyer went mad then, shrieking in its excruciating agony, worm-body coiling and whipping, flinging its harshly gibbering Rider down onto the white sand. Crow had but a second to collect his scattered senses as the dazed and suddenly silenced Rider climbed to its feet, but in that second he saw his sword sticking pommel-up from a patch of slimed sand.

The weapon lay directly in the path of the Runner, which was again heading, in an erratic and lumbering fashion, for the gore-spattered dreamer. Crow saw the thing's approach as a last desperate effort to bring him down before the seepage of its vile life's juices stilled it forever; he saw, too, the possible destruction of his sword beneath that lopsidedly pounding hammer-leg.

Without the scimitar he was done for, and so he hurled himself frantically across the sand, fingers stretched wide and reaching. Even as his hand grasped the hilt of the curving sword, Crow knew he had run out of time. The huge, pounding leg of the Runner was already in the air, its own thrust compensating for the missing outer member. Down came that great hammer toward his head – and then, a miracle!

With a bubbling shriek something shot over Crow's

spread-eagled body on tortured wings to smack blindly into the towering Runner. Bat-worm and Runner alike crashed down onto the sand as Crow rose with the scimitar in his hand, unable to believe that he still lived. The Runner lay there – mad fangs gnashing in its hideous face, its remaining outer leg limp but its hammer continuing to pound away at the air – and the half-crippled Flyer flopped mindlessly about on the sand, its fractured beak dripping evil-smelling liquid.

The dreamer knew suddenly the means by which that bat-worm had known his whereabouts during the fight. The thing had somehow been guided by its Rider – that Rider which held the reins *in its mind* rather than in its hand! The two had existed in a weird symbiosis. But now, without its Rider, the Flyer was truly blind! No wonder the tentacled Rider was even now crying out harshly to the wounded monster, trying the while to climb once more onto its back.

'To hell with that!' Crow roared, leaping forward to swing his sword in an awesome blow that cut into and through the neck of the bat-worm, sending its evil head flying to spatter the already fouled sand. Yet again the half-mounted Rider fell as the body of his beast-brother commenced its last, convulsive spasm and fell to sprawl on the white sand beside the now motionless Runner.

And now the Rider saw that he was indeed on his own. With an alien cry of rage and hatred he sprang to his feet, uncoiling his tentacular arms, drawing them back whiplike onto the sand behind him. Crow knew that in another moment those viciously claw-tipped weapons would be at him; his superb reactions took over almost unbidden. In one lithe movement he leaned forward, throwing the scimitar like a knife straight at the Rider's black heart.

The point ran home and the weight of the curving blade carried it through the Rider's thin body. Surprise grew like a pale stain on the creature's face, then his tentacular arms wrapped themselves spastically around the length of his body, head to toe. The hideous form trembled violently for a moment and gave one final shriek of hatred and frustration before falling slowly over backward onto the churned and stained sand. In a count of ten, bar the dreamer's hoarse shout of triumph, the white cavern was still again and silent.

For a few seconds more Titus Crow swayed over the bodies of the defeated trio, every flesh-and-blood muscle in his body aching and his arms like lead. Then he lifted his eyes to peer undaunted across the white waste. Somewhere here, somewhere in this glaring white nightmare, Tiania of Elysia was even now in dire need of him.

He had not a moment to spare.

4

The Clock in Flames!

Three hours had elapsed in Dylath-Leen since Henri-Laurent de Marigny's disappearance from the dais of the ruby. During the interval there had been some little turmoil in the city. Barzt, the new, self-appointed leader of the horned ones, had himself very recently been removed from power. His position had been disputed; a fight with knives had decided the matter positively in favor of his opponent. That opponent, Eriff, now licked his wounds and supped muth-dew with his cronies in a rotting tavern near the seafront.

There was much for Eriff to consider now that he was a leader; a good deal of thinking – an art for which he had no great aptitude – was required. He was uncertain now, for example, whether or not his usurping of Barzt's pretensions to leadership of the horned ones had been a wise move. Nyarlathotep was coming to Dylath-Leen, expecting to interrogate (whatever form such interrogation might take) the man and woman of the waking world. That prize pair, however, were no longer here. Even the unknown dreamer who freed them had made his escape, albeit into oblivion. On top of all this, disturbing reports were beginning to reach the horned ones in their basalt city, reports hinting that the insidious incursions of their agents into the healthier cities of dreamland were being inexplicably checked, particularly in Ulthar, which had been their next objective.

No, Eriff was not at all happy with the situation, and what little he knew of Nyarlathotep only went to increase his apprehension. Perhaps it were better, he was beginning to reason, that the ancient compact between the horned ones of Leng and the prisoned Great Old Ones of the Cthulhu Cycle had never been. Better, perhaps, if all of Dylath-Leen's horned ones now took to their black galleys and sailed away across the Southern Sea. Better for Eriff, certainly; for what had he now to offer that mighty emissary of Cthulhu, the dread Nyarlathotep? Utterly emptyhanded, how might he greet the Great Messenger?

So Eriff grumbled over his muth-dew and nursed his bruises and cuts. And this was the brooding, pensive mood he was in when they came from the square of the great ruby to find him, bringing him the news that even now a strange, silent, enigmatic visitor stood in Dylath-Leen's central square on the cobbles opposite the ruby dais. The thing, they said, was tall and oddly figured, like a mummycase of olden Ohlmi. Of wood or a material like wood, it was very heavy and hard, and in its upper part four hands swung about a common center in wholly inexplicable motions. Would Eriff not come and say what must be done with this object, which had appeared as if from thin air?

In the heat of the afternoon Eriff left his cool drink and made his way with his retinue of cronies painfully to the square of the ruby dais. And it was just as he had heard it: there, facing the dais almost as if it scrutinized the monstrous ruby atop the basalt steps, stood the unknown object from another world. Eriff, for all his ignorance, saw one thing immediately: that indeed this thing was not fashioned of dreamland's skills. Staring at the time-clock, his unnatural features quickly took on a cautious, a suspicious look.

How did this thing get here? What was it? Why was it here in the square of the ruby? He had been told that it was of wood, and certainly it appeared to be. Well then, why take chances?

'Either carry it away, out of the city, or burn it!' he ordered. 'Use old timbers, doors, and furniture from the city's houses. Build a pyre for the thing, whatever it is. I don't like it . . .'

'But Eriff, it appears to be a box of some sort!' one of his brothers protested.

'And what's inside it?' he asked.

'We don't know, but –'

'And can you open it?'

'Not yet, but –'

'Then burn it and be on the safe side!'

And so a pyre was built around the time-clock, of furniture from the old uninhabited houses and timbers from other habitations long fallen into ruin; and when the time-clock was completely obscured from view by the flammable materials thus heaped about it, then torches were brought and the fire lighted.

Within the clock, whose shell was impervious to all but the most incredible temperatures and pressures, in an indeterminate limbo which might best be described as the place where all the 'corners' of space and time meet, Henri-Laurent de Marigny was ill. He was as drunk, more drunk than at any previous time in his entire life. That is not to say that he had never before consumed a whole bottle of brandy – he had, but in a civilized manner. Never in such barbarous haste!

And yet he knew that he had a mission . . . if only this dark universe would stop revolving long enough to allow him to remember what that mission was! It had to do with Titus Crow, and it had to do with Tiania . . . And with the time-clock.

The time-clock! De Marigny's mind fastened avidly upon that concept.

Time-clock! Of course! He was *inside* that peculiar device, that space-time vehicle, right now – in a warm womb between the worlds. He had only to reach out his mind, and – but that would be too much of an effort. It would be better simply to fight the flooding nausea within himself, the sickening spinning and whirling of vast black voids within and without him. Oh, yes – much better to sleep until the alcohol had burned itself out of his system.

Alcohol?

Sleep . . .?

Alarm bells clamored distantly in de Marigny's inner being. Alcohol – sleep – *dream!* That had been his mission: to sleep and to dream. And he had slept, he knew that. Why, then, was he not dreaming?

The answer was obvious: he was not dreaming because as he had fallen drunkenly asleep he had released his mental contact with the time-clock. Where was the clock now? Had he in fact managed to pilot his fantastic vehicle to the desired destination?

Now he put himself to the effort so recently rejected, meshing his besotted mind with that of his machine – and instantly the scanners opened in his mind's eye.

An inferno – all the fires of hell blazing about the clock – the inner cone of some primeval volcano during an eruption – the fiery surface of the solar orb itself! *Where the devil was he?*

Panic clawed momentarily at de Marigny's insides as he instinctively threw up his arms to ward off the heat that he knew could never penetrate the clock's shell. Then, fleetingly through the flame and smoke, he glimpsed the ruby dais and the horned figures that cavorted around the bonfire in demoniac glee, and he knew where he was. He was back in Dylath-Leen, in Earth's dreamland. Now too, however drunkenly, he remembered what had gone before.

Then, fighting to hold the time-clock's scanners steady in his staggering mind, de Marigny attempted to focus his blurred thoughts on the horned ones, on their present activity. What were they doing now, these wide-mouthed monsters? Plainly, they were trying to burn the time-clock! Anger began to expand within de Marigny's breast. He glared at the creatures from Leng with a fiery hatred that burned in his veins to match the heat of the brandy.

These vile inhabitants of the forbidden plateau had perpetrated enough horrors in the lands of Earth's dreams. They, or their fathers before them, had brought down Dylath-Leen in the first place; they were responsible for the dissemination of much that was abominable in dreamland; they were the foul sores of Man's subconscious, in league with the Powers of Darkness, particularly with the prisoned Cthulhu spawn of the waking world. And on top of all this they had recently humiliated Titus Crow, Tiania, even de Marigny himself.

Tiania they would have violated – unthinkably. Crow would have been put to terrible tortures; indeed, de Marigny's friends would eventually have been handed over to Nyarlathotep, the Great Messenger of the CCD. And here in dreamland Nyarlathotep had been given monstrous form by the massed telepathic sendings of his immemorial masters. The more the dreamer's foggy mind dwelled on the CCD – and on the horned ones, their minions in dreamland – the more angry he became. And now those minions were trying to burn the time-clock, with de Marigny inside it!

His anger suddenly boiled over into a rage that drove back his alcoholic nausea and brought him into awesome action. It was high time these Leng-spawned horrors were taught a lesson, and one that would not be quickly forgotten . . .

Weapon from the Waking World

It was, of course, the habit of the horned ones of Leng – who were cannibals whenever the opportunity to eat the flesh of sentient beings presented itself – to leap and dance about their ritual fires. In this way in ages long lost they had thought to propitiate the elemental spirits. Therefore, the knowledge that an enemy – a thing alien to their monstrous conception of normalcy, in the shape of the time-clock – was burning in the center of their bonfire was sufficient to set them dancing. Had they been roasting a man, then they would have leaped in time to his screaming, invoking the spirits of the feast. In the case of the clock, they danced to thank the spirits of their fathers, which had delivered this enemy unto them.

Eriff, lightly wounded in his fight with the unfortunate Barzt, sat on the steps of the ruby dais and clapped his hands, accompanying the musicians who rattled chalk-dry crotala and played upon whining flutes. All the while, other horned ones darted in and out between the encircling dancers, feeding the flames with the looted furniture of olden Dylath-Leen.

Then there was an astounding occurrence: the strange, coffin-shaped object at the fire's core started to spin, fanning the flames of the fire outward.

Instantly the dancers backed away, the dreadful caco-phony of the musicians faded, and Eriff stopped his clapping to stand up on the dais steps, his too-wide mouth falling open and his slanted eyes bugging. Faster the time-clock whirled, until a wind began to roar outward from it that hurled blazing brands in all directions. Now the horned ones broke and scattered, screaming and gibbering, many of them beating frantically at themselves as their coarse silken clothes caught fire.

And up rose the spinning clock from the blackened cobbles, the winds of its whirling bowling over the fleeing horned ones, hurling great timbers about like straws, its shrieking voice that of the storm-demon and its wild gyrations increasing from moment to moment. Then, high above the square, it tilted, seeming to aim itself directly at the basalt dais – at the massive ruby!

Finally Eriff, recovering his slow wits, made to flee from the steps of the dais – but too late. Such was the speed of the clock as it drilled down through tortured air to slam into, *through* the splintering jewel, that for a second it seemed simply to elongate itself.

Eriff was shredded as he tried to run from the steps, blasted into crimson pieces by the bombburst of ruby fragments; and the clock drove on, wildly slewing to one side, tearing a great hole in one of the square's buildings before coming to a shuddering halt in the debris. For a moment or two there was silence in the square of the dais.

Within the clock de Marigny fought down the rising tide of nausea within him, a sickness born not only of his alcoholic condition but also of the devastation he had wrought in the space of the last few seconds. For of course he had seen the results of his great anger, and drunk or sober such slaughter was not to de Marigny's liking. Not now that his original passion of rage was dying down. It was one thing to do away with such as the three who had so direly threatened Titus Crow and Tiania when they were tied to the dais steps, even coldbloodedly, but quite another to go unaffected by the scene in the square as it was now.

Corpses literally littered the smeared and slimed cobbles, many of them with limbs missing, torn like Eriff in the explosion of ruby shards; others lay in smoldering rags or trapped beneath still-burning timbers. And there were some who still lived, crawling across the square, mewling dementedly both in fear and in the agony of their wounds . . .

Finally, shakily, de Marigny took control of the clock once more, freeing it from the rubble of the collapsed wall and turning it toward the now empty dais. As he did so he saw several of the horned ones, apparently unharmed, climbing to their feet and backing away in utmost horror from the center of the square. At first he could not make out what it was that they so patently feared. It was not de Marigny's coffin-shaped weapon from the waking world; indeed, they appeared to be ignoring the time-clock completely. Then –

There atop the dais steps, shimmering faintly in the cleansing sunlight, a shape gathered. Even as he focused the clock's scanners upon the thing, its form began to solidify, its outline to fill in. And at last de Marigny knew what the thing was.

The Fly-the-Light from Yuggoth on the Rim – a vampire molded of the malignity of the Cthulhu Cycle Deities themselves – a thing of *Their* manufacture! In shattering the great ruby, he had freed the demon from that multifaceted prison, loosing it for the second time upon Dylath-Leen . . . except that this time the sunlight poured down upon it from a clear mid-afternoon sky, the blessed light from which it must either flee or die!

De Marigny saw the horror, but still could hardly believe his own eyes. He remembered Grant Enderby's ambiguous description and knew now why the man had phrased it so. For how might one describe this monster except as Enderby had described it? Blind and yet all-seeing – limbless and yet mobile as some vast, mercurial amoeba – with poisonous mouths that gaped and drooled in its bubbling mass! The only thing

Enderby had left out of his tale was the thing's size. It was *huge!*

And it was screaming – shrieking and writhing in agony under the rays of the sun – melting and shrinking visibly as great black clouds of smoke poured from it. Then it 'saw' the half-dozen or so horned ones that cringed away from it as they tried to slink unseen from the square. And it was just as Enderby had said: the Fly-the-Light moved after them like flood water, pouring down the dais steps and soaking them up in an instant. When the frantic, awful screaming had stopped, finally the thing 'saw' the time-clock.

By then its bulk was greatly reduced, despite the *sustenance* so recently and hideously derived from the six or seven horned ones, whose bones now gleamed wetly in small heaps about the square. Black smoke still roiled from it; its quakings were awful to watch; the screaming sounds it made had risen so far up the sonic scale as to be almost inaudible. And yet, when the horror suddenly made for the time-clock, de Marigny sensed that it was far from done for. He sensed, too, that the thing knew what the time-clock was, its fantastic function. The vampire had purpose now, its movements were no longer hopeless; it seemed to exude an essence of eager – anticipation!

Then an incredible suspicion set de Marigny's flesh to creeping. What if this thing of blackest nightmare was capable of entering into the time-clock? Suppose it could *come through* the clock's outer shell? Titus Crow had told him that the Hounds of Tindalos could do this quite effortlessly. Was it completely inconceivable that this thing from the great ruby might possess the same power? De Marigny in no way intended to put his suspicion to the test. He backed his vehicle hurriedly away as the Fly-the-Light rushed upon him, lifting the vessel up high into the sunlight over the square in an effort to avoid contact with the horror.

He was astounded and terrified when the vampire flashed skyward after him! The thing did not recognize the restrictions of gravity!

By now it was much smaller – a pulsating fireball of greenly drooling mouths that trailed a pall of foul black smoke. But it moved at a lightning pace that de Marigny, still drunk and completely off guard, found difficulty in matching. It was not that the clock could not outrun the vampire, rather that the man within the clock was off guard, by no means recovered yet from his overdose of alcohol.

Then, his dulled senses shocked into positive action, at last de Marigny made to flee the Fly-the-Light's advances at full speed – only to discover that the demon was not prepared to let him go! A numbness fell over his mind like an icy shroud; a great white fog obscured his brain; and pouring from behind this awful mental mist, penetrating it, came the mind-commands of the thing from the ruby:

'You will not flee. Stand and accept me. You have not the strength to flee. You are weak, as all mortal creatures are weak, and I am strong. Even now I am stronger than you, but I will be mighty once more. Therefore you must obey me. Stand – you may not flee – you have not the strength to flee!'

Over and over the message repeated in de Marigny's mind, and while he was dimly aware of what was happening, still the dreadful paralysis held him in an unbreakable embrace. This was that debilitating force with which the ruby-creature had whelmed Dylath-Leen's peoples many years ago, the vampiric power that had drained even Titus Crow of his strength. And now, freed from the prisoning ruby, the former gem-dweller was concentrating that power in its last bid for life.

The thing was depleted and quickly dying, but still the mental sloth it generated gripped de Marigny's mind as it moved, carefully now, toward the time-clock. And the

139

paralyzed dreamer knew that indeed the clock would be the horror's salvation, for once inside the weird vehicle – and as soon as its present master had been dealt with – then the thing would be truly free to ravage among all the dark dimensions of a limitless multiverse. That must never be.

As the horror closed with him, de Marigny groped for the clock's controls with blunted senses. It was quite hopeless. He could find nothing. The time-clock was completely immobilized. The Fly-the-Light sensed this too, and thrust itself triumphantly upon its prey in one last surge of waning strength. In that final moment, still desperately groping in vague, unfeeling abysses, de Marigny came across a control which had absolutely nothing to do with the clock's mobility. It was a trigger rather than a control proper, the trigger that powered a weapon Titus Crow had brought back with him from Elysis!

De Marigny squeezed that trigger.

Instantly the alien numbness was flushed from his mind. The vampire dwindled in his scanners, dwindled and boiled as a beam of purest light flashed from the clock's dial to strike it squarely and thrust it back. The beam lengthened as it forced the shrinking horror away, until finally the dying thing was pinned by that shaft of light to the basalt dais amidst shards of shattered ruby.

There, at last, in a blaze of purest white light, the creature expired, became nothing. And still de Marigny played his weapon's beam upon the spot where it had been. Shortly the dais itself began to melt and bubble, the very basalt to run like water. Only then, when the dais was a misshapen hummock of glowing rock, did de Marigny release the mental trigger.

Wearily then, thankfully, the dreamer set the clock down in the silent, scorched square. And yet, exhausted as he now felt and still by no means sober, he remembered Titus Crow and Tiania. Indeed they were now uppermost

140

in his thoughts. What terrors were they facing even now? And what was he doing, wasting his time here in Dylath-Leen?

He grasped his vehicle's controls with his mind and lifted it up, however tiredly, unsteadily, to the skies. But where to go? Where was Titus Crow now?

No sooner had the unspoken question passed through de Marigny's mind than the clock trembled and strained like a great hound tugging at its leash, and simultaneously a scene of startling clarity flashed upon the dreamer's inner eye. He saw Titus Crow, naked, pacing a great white sandy expanse, scimitar in hand, head hung low. The vision began to fade – but not before Crow had looked up startled, frowning and peering puzzledly about.

His face was dusted with white sand, caked at the corners of his mouth, and his weariness was plainly great. Even as the vision receded once more and vanished from de Marigny's mind, he saw Crow's lips form the question: 'Henri! Is that you?'

And de Marigny *knew!*

Of course! There had always existed between the two men a strange psychic link – a connection which the time-clock had momentarily picked up and magnified. Indeed, this was how Titus Crow had found his way back to Earth from Elysia, by using de Marigny's mind as a beacon. Well, why shouldn't the method work just as well in reverse?

He released his mental grasp upon the clock's controls by all but the merest contact, then transmitted the following message to that vehicle of the Elder Gods: 'You know where Crow is. He's here within my mind – within *our* minds! – and he's in trouble. It's up to you now. Go to him – *go to Titus Crow!*'

And like a great hound hearing its master's call, freed from the restraining leash, away the clock raced across the skies of dreamland . . .

6

At the Pits of Nightmare

The white sand tugged at Titus Crow's naked feet; fine particles of white dust stung his eyes and clogged his nostrils. His scimitar seemed to weigh a ton and he felt as though he had walked a thousand miles. He allowed himself a derisive snort and cursed whichever fool had said that things were often far simpler in dreams. If that were really so, then it was high time things began working in favor of Titus Crow!

For hours now – or what seemed like hours – he had been making his way toward what looked like a continuous geyser of concentric rings of steam or vapor, rising, expanding, and dispersing high in the atmosphere of the great cave. He had first seen this phenomenon shortly after setting out across the desert and had automatically headed toward it. These distant smoke rings, rolling swiftly up at regular intervals from some unknown source, had been the only sign of life, however inorganic, in the entire cavern. His instinct told him that this was where he would find Tiania.

And at long last he had almost reached his destination. Just across a range of low dunes lay the source of these puzzling eruptions of vapor. The sand now transmitted to his naked feet a steady hammering as of massive subterranean sledges, and he saw that the rising rings of vapor soared skyward in perfect synchronization with these poundings. These were not, Crow was certain, purely natural phenomena. Then, mounting the crest, he saw how right his instinct had been.

The scene was alien and fantastic. Beyond the dunes a

deep valley opened to Crow's eyes; in its center a crater, with sides of fused sand, went down like the mouth of some vast funnel into indeterminate abysses of earth. To one side of this gaping hole, from which issued the billowing smoke rings, a structure like some enormous asymetrical birdcage stood, of intertwining metal bars half rotten with a leprous gray oxidization. Within the cage, which was open at its very top, a motley collection of dreamland's diverse peoples, men, women, and children, stood or reclined upon the sandy floor. Many of them were plainly distraught, wringing their hands and crying out in horror at their plight, beating frenziedly with bloodied hands at the metal bars of their prison. Others simply lay on the sand in attitudes of exhaustion, or sat blankly staring at nothing through eyes glazed with shock.

There were other . . . *things* . . . to be seen: the Keeper of the Cage, for instance, seated on a throne of boulders; and the great gaunt, perched now upon the Keeper's shoulder. But for the moment Crow's eyes sought elsewhere. They swept the crowded cage until finally they rested upon Tiania. And within that singular prison she was even now in danger of hideous outrage!

Two horned ones were trapped in the cage along with all the rest, and they were trying to dislodge Tiania from where she clung halfway up the cage's wall in a latticework of silver bars. They were climbing after her, laughing loudly and gutturally as they snatched at her naked feet to bring her down.

All common sense, all caution went out of Titus Crow then. Strength born of a raging bloodlust surged in his veins and the purr of his synthetic heart became a snarl deep within his chest. His cry of rage was almost animal; he saw nothing but blood – the blood of the horned ones from Leng – as he raced with all speed down the dune. He ignored utterly, as if they did not exist, the creatures that kept the cage. Skirting the crater, running like the wind, he came to the cage and put his terrible strength to bear upon the bars where they seemed most rotten. In a rending of rusted metal he was inside the cage, leaping the prostrate forms of weeping inmates and dodging the beseeching embrace of others as he raced across the sandy floor.

Another moment saw him directly beneath the horned ones who climbed after Tiania; and then, because he could not climb and carry his scimitar easily at the same time, he put down the sword and swung himself swiftly up into the framework of bars. By now the horned ones had seen him – Tiania, too.

'Be careful, Titus!' she cried.

Dodging a kick from the lower of the two horned ones, he grabbed the creature's leg and hauled mightily. The thing from Leng gave a shriek and tried to hold on to the bars; Crow shook him like a hawk shakes its prey, tore him loose and threw him down to the floor fifty feet below. Then, hauling himself higher, he came face to face with the second of Tiania's tormentors.

The horned one had made himself fast in a secure position; he stabbed at Crow with a curving knife. Crow caught the creature's wrist, twisting until its snarls became cries of pain. Then he swiftly twisted the other way, slamming an elbow of hard flesh with a core of harder bone and plastic into the horned one's face.

That face was smashed in an instant. Teeth crunched and blood flew. The nose disintegrated, the wide mouth became a red gash, the slanting eyes glazed over. Crow released his grip on the horned one's wrist, caught him by his neck, and jerked him free of the bars into empty air. A moment later came the crunch of bones from below. Then Crow reached for Tiania where she clung naked to the bars just a few feet higher.

Before their hands could meet there came a buffeting of air and a shadow fell across them. Crow cried out a sick denial as the great gaunt soared down through the open roof of the cage to snatch the girl from her precarious position. Tiania screamed and struggled as she was lifted up, up and out of the cage, carried high into the white cavern's atmosphere. There the great gaunt found the thermal current rising from the crater and glided in wide circles in the rising air. Below the gaunt where it soared with its wriggling captive, the smoke rings went down in concentric circles to the crater-like vent that issued them; the thundering, as of massive, monstrous engines, pounded up through leagues of earth and sand to make the very air shimmer and vibrate.

With horrified eyes Titus Crow watched the circling gaunt, certain with every passing moment that the blank-faced bat-thing would drop Tiania into the throat of the mysterious vent. Then the Keeper of the Cage spoke:

'Come down from the cage, man of the waking world. Come and speak to me.' The voice of the gigantic, manlike figure was loud to match its dimensions but flat and utterly void of life. It was as if some colossal zombie had spoken, a thing brought back from the dead against its will, without emotion.

Titus Crow dragged his eyes from the high-circling gaunt and stared at the Keeper where it sat upon its throne of huge boulders. It was as naked as Crow himself, hairless, with skin the color of death. Its eyes were lusterless yellow orbs that never blinked, through which it seemed to stare straight into Crow's very soul.

'I'll come down,' Crow shouted his answer, clambering down the bars of the cage, 'and I'll speak to you – but order your hideous pet to bring my woman down to safety!'

'Your woman? No, she is mine now, and when I am ready she will go down into darkness to fuel the nightmares of certain awful dreamers. You, too, are destined for the pits of nightmare. But not until I have spoken with you.'

By then Crow had left the cage through the hole he'd made in its rotten bars. He ran to the feet of the Keeper of the Cage and waved his scimitar futilely up at the giant. 'Why?' he shouted. 'Why will you do these things?'

'It is my reason for being. It is why *They* put me here. Long and long ago I was a man of the waking world, like you. But I learned the mysteries of the Great Old Ones and became *Their* priest. Then, when I tried to use *Their* power to my own ends, *They* destroyed me on Earth and put me here to serve *Them* in Earth's dreamland. *They* gave me great size and amazing powers to command. Then, mockingly, *They* robbed me of my will, left me emotionless. I am almost omnipotent, almost immortal, and yet I am *Their* slave, powerless to do except as *They* will be done.' Even saying these things the huge figure showed no emotion; the tone of his voice remained unvaried.

'If the Cthulhu spawn did these things to you, then Cthulhu is your enemy no less than mine,' Crow cried. 'Yet you have given yourself over into his service – you are his slave. I would sooner die than be slave to Cthulhu, but I'll fight as long as there's life in me!'

The Keeper answered: 'Ah, but *They* thought of that, too. I might also fight, might also believe death preferable to this existence *They* plotted for me – had *They* not increased tenfold within me the human instinct for survival. All I have is an unquenchable desire to survive – and to survive I must obey.'

With that the massive, white-fleshed creature leaned forward and scooped up Titus Crow in one hand before he could move. Crow struck time and again at the great hand that held him, but his blade drew no blood from the deathly flesh.

'Now,' the Keeper continued, 'stop your pointless striving and tell me who you are, why you are so different from other men. You are strong beyond belief for a mortal dreamer, and strange, too, I fancy.'

'And if I tell you these things will you set the woman free?'

'No, no. You and she must both go down to nightmare. Down there in the pit, where the Engines of Horror pound, your souls will feed the darkest dreams of the Great Old Ones, and the nightmares *They* send to plague human dreamers will be that much more horrible.'

'Then I'll not speak to you. I'll speak only to . . . Nyarlathotep!' Crow cried, desperately.

'Nyarlathotep?' No emotion but a certain hesitation entered into the Keeper's voice. 'What do you want with Nyarlathotep – and what makes you think that the Great Messenger would want anything of you?'

'He wants to . . . to see us,' Crow insisted. 'I don't know why.'

'If what you say is true, then I was right and you are indeed an extraordinary human being. I believe you.' With that, the Keeper lifted up a great dead white arm and beckoned, and the circling gaunt immediately flew down and settled on his shoulder, still holding fast to the wriggling form of Tiania.

'I have the power,' the Keeper continued, 'to contact *Them* in *Their* immemorial slumbers. Perhaps *They* will send Nyarlathotep directly to see you.'

'No!' Crow gasped.

'Oh? Were you after all lying, then?'

'No, but –'

'But you don't really want to see Nyarlathotep? I see. His plans for you are not to your liking, that is it. I will contact *Them*. But meanwhile my familiar must be about his work. See, you have freed all of my prisoners. They have escaped through the hole you tore in the cage's bars.'

Crow saw that the Keeper was right. The last of the

escapees was just hurrying over the crest of the sandhills out of sight. Again the Keeper gave a signal, and Tiania fell from the great gaunt's clutches and slid with a cry of alarm down over the Keeper's leprous chest and onto his lap.

The Keeper placed Crow in his lap, too, and at that moment, as the great gaunt flapped aloft to soar after the fleeing people from the cage – then came an amazing diversion!

7

Dreams of a Diseased Mind

Out of the sky, from above the white horizon of sandhills, a beam of purest white light struck at the great gaunt, shredding one wing into a swirling gray mist of fine particles. The beam was cut off instantly at its as yet unseen source, leaving the crippled gaunt to spin madly down, down the funnel of concentric smoke rings to where it struck the curving mouth of the pit, bouncing and tumbling like a bundle of rags before plummeting out of sight into the abyss. And not once did the creature voice its agony; no cry escaped it as it went down to the pits of nightmare.

'Whatever this is,' said the Keeper, 'plainly it is not intended to benefit me. Someone seeks perhaps to rescue you, or to destroy me, or both. If the intention is to rescue you, then your rescuer must first destroy me. Therefore I give your would-be rescuer no chance!' Even as the vast pale creature spoke – even as he snatched up Titus Crow and Tiania in one massive hand, holding them high over the throat of the great pit – so the white beam came again, lancing out of the sky to strike him square in his leprous chest.

The Keeper sprang to his feet and reeled at the edge of the pit. His strange eyes stood out huge and round in his face, and from his suddenly scarred and seared chest there came a deep and plainly audible wheezing. Now he slowly opened his outstretched hand, so that the dreamers had to scramble up onto his palm, clinging to each other above the vapor-belching pit.

'If he strikes me again, whoever or whatever he is, then

he strikes all three of us,' the Keeper said, pain in his voice but still no emotion. 'For you will fall as surely as I, but you will fall into deepest purgatory. You see? It is my instinct for survival . . .'

By now the time-clock was plainly visible, racing in wide circles at some considerable height above the cage and its Keeper. Titus Crow knew that only Henri-Laurent de Marigny could be at the machine's controls, and hope sprang up in him as he watched its circlings. The Keeper followed Crow's eyes to the clock and he asked: 'What kind of device is that?'

'Right now it's a weapon,' Crow answered. 'From the waking world. A weapon against all the Cthulhu Cycle Deities and their minions!'

'You are . . . stranger than I thought, dreamer,' the vast being said, his voice now faltering, an echoing croak that crackled like muted lightning. His great palm, upon which Crow and Tiania crouched, trembled mightily. They threw themselves down to lie prone across the huge fingers.

Suddenly the Keeper fell to his knees, the ground trembling as all the tons of his weight crashed down upon the sand. But still he held out his hand, palm up, above the great glassy abyss. Now the time-clock was stationary, poised threateningly on high, its dial turned toward the fantastic tableau below.

There at the lip of the infernal funnel, from whose nightmare throat those exhalations of obscene vapor puffed upward unabatedly, the Keeper kneeled, plainly injured. Crow and Tiania hung on grimly to his great fingers as his huge frame trembled, rocking to and fro. Beside him the now empty cage was an oddly woven lobster pot of gleaming metal and scabrous gray rust, and on all sides the white sand formed a dazzling, sterile backdrop to the entire scene. The time-clock fell from on high, moved closer, and became motionless again.

'It is my belief,' came the Keeper's broken voice,

drawing Crow's fevered gaze back from the time-clock, 'that for all your woman's strange beauty you, dreamer, are far more important in the great scheme of things. That being so, I will now let her fall into nightmare, saving you until later. But unless you send your aerial weapon away, you will surely follow her.'

'If you let her fall,' Crow shouted, a conflicting mixture of horror, rage, and desperation in his voice, 'I'll order your death immediately!'

'And your own?'

Crow knew what the Keeper meant: if the white ray struck him down, then Crow must fall from his hand into the pit. He answered, 'And my own.'

'Bluff.' The Keeper's free hand moved out over the pit, thumb and forefinger reaching for Tiania. She threw her arms about her man.

'Wait!' Crow slashed uselessly at the threatening fingers with his scimitar. 'Even if I were bluffing, what about Nyarlathotep? He wants to see us. Had you forgotten? Even if you escape with your miserable life – if my weapon from the waking world fails to kill you – how will you explain the woman's death, my death, to your masters?'

'Her death? Oh, but she will not . . . die, not immediately, not for a . . . long time. You do not . . . know as much as you . . . pretend, dreamer,' the Keeper wheezed shudderingly on. 'Nyarlathotep is . . . *Their* messenger, the Great . . . Messenger of my masters. Embodied or . . . disembodied, he is . . . *Their* messenger.

'Ask yourself who it is that carries Cthulhu's nightmares to . . . influence the dreams of mortals. It is . . . Nyarlathotep! You desired to . . . see him? So you shall – at the pits of nightmare. There your souls will fuel the engines of horror, for long and long before . . . you are . . . finished; and Nyarlathotep will disseminate all the . . . horror of your shrieking minds and souls among the dreams of . . . other mortals. But enough! The woman first!'

Suddenly Tiania, breathless and frightened but brave as ever, freed herself from Crow's arms to throw back her emerald hair in a defiant gesture. Her beautiful voice trembled almost unnoticeably as she spoke up in her own right.

'You would do this to Tiania of Elysia? Then you are surely doomed in this land of dream and in all others. You should know, creature, that I am beloved of the Elder Gods – beloved of Kthanid himself. Beware!'

'The . . . Elder Gods? Kthanid?' For the first time there was, or appeared to be, a trace of emotion – fear – in the Keeper's steadily disintegrating voice. 'You are of . . . Elysia?'

The vast being's frame rocked more wildly yet, and for a moment his hand swung to one side, so that the pair huddled upon his palm suddenly found themselves above sandy ground and not the gaping maw of the glassy-throated pit. In one movement Crow grabbed Tiania and carried her into space in a coiled-spring leap; and in that same instant de Marigny, seizing upon his one opportunity, applied pressure to the mental trigger that controlled the time-clock's weapon.

Again the white ray reached blindingly, unerringly out, stabbing at the Keeper and striking him between the eyes. He fell back upon his haunches, clawing at his face and jerking spastically, toppling against the cage, which crumpled beneath his great weight.

Titus Crow hit the ground a second later, holding Tiania above him, deliberately cushioning her with his body as she fell upon him. It was a fall of at least thirty feet and would certainly have broken the bones of any normal man. Crow was not normal, however, and had fallen in a spot where the sand was soft and deep. Nevertheless, he was momentarily winded, so that it was several seconds before he drew himself to his knees to take the badly shaken Tiania in his arms. They had been lucky: a distance of only a few feet separated them from the smooth, curving lip of the pit, from which those regular exhalations went up inexorably as ever to the great cavern's roof. There, at the edge of the pit, clinging together, they saw a terrible sight.

The time-clock, flying in tight circles about the Keeper's gigantic, leprous, reeling form, was pouring a constant beam of white light down upon him, and wherever the ray struck his body oily black smoke gushed out from steaming pits to form darkly drifting cloudlets in the throbbing air.

It could not last for long. With one abrupt, flailing motion, the mortally wounded Keeper lurched to his feet. He glared from a single bulging eye – its twin now a gaping, blackly bubbling hole – and took a single, stumbling step after his aerial tormentor. Then he swayed to a halt. His mouth fell open and he spoke, signaling at last his recognition of doom, the fact that for all his instinct for survival, his lust for life even in the hell that Cthulhu had given him, he was done for.

'I know this . . . *power!*' he cried, his voice a monstrous bell with a cracked clapper, tolling a cacophony of horror. 'I . . . know it. It is . . . that power which . . . even *They* fear. It is . . . the star of Mnar – the love of the . . . Elder Gods – the Good before which all Evil . . . flees. And it is . . . my . . . death!'

He staggered wildly, then spun about, throwing his arms wide to form an unholy cross. And again the beam of white light reached out. But this time de Marigny aimed it out of mercy. The beam played upon, passed *through* the Keeper's body, finally expending its potent energies harmlessly in the sand. The giant uttered one last incoherent cry; his arms fell uselessly to his sides; his head snapped back with a loud crack. He toppled forward, it seemed almost in slow-motion, crashing headlong down the glassy funnel to hell.

Titus Crow and Tiania, fleeing wearily toward the sandhills, were hurled flat by the hurricane rush of displaced air and stinging sand as the colossus fell. When they regained their feet again he was gone, and for several minutes there were no more rings of vapor rising over the white sands . . .

Cresting the dunes, they came to where de Marigny stood at the open door of the time-clock. He was deathly pale, trembling; he leaned unsteadily, balancing himself by holding onto the clock.

'Henri,' Crow said, taking his arm. 'Without you we were finished. You'll never know how I felt when . . .' His voice tapered off and a frown creased his brow. He put his face closer to de Marigny's and sniffed suspiciously. The frown deepened. 'Man, I do believe you're drunk!'

'No, no, Titus,' the other managed a sickly grin. 'I'm almost sober now. But you should have seen me an hour or so ago! Here.' He passed Crow an unopened bottle of brandy. 'I don't care if I never taste a drop again.'

'What? Brandy?' Crow turned to Tiania and hugged her, showing her the bottle. 'Even in Elysia there's nothing quite like this, Tiania. What a man, eh? Twice he's rescued me in ten minutes!' Then his voice took on a more serious note. 'But we'll celebrate later. Right now all I want to do is –'

At that moment there came a deep subterranean rumbling that shook the ground and made the trio stumble to keep their balance. It seemed suddenly darker, as though clouds had gathered to obscure the sun, though no such healthy orb illumined the great cavern. Again the ground shuddered, and they felt a series of dull detonations far below. A moment more and there came a roaring blast from the mouth of the pit, and almost simultaneously a huge black ring of smoke hurtled up into view – and with it the vilest stench imaginable.

'Right now,' said de Marigny, finishing what Crow had started to say, 'I reckon we ought to be getting out of here!'

Crow nodded in agreement, bundled de Marigny in through the clock's open panel and Tiania after him, looked once more upon the awful landscape of the white underworld, whose light was now visibly failing, then entered the clock himself.

As he took the vessel's familiar controls and lifted it up into the cave's atmosphere, Crow saw massive cracks opening in the floor of the desert. Dimly in the distance he perceived through the clock's scanners the impending death of this subterranean vault: the fall of great chunks of rock, stalactites and smaller debris from the shuddering ceiling. Of the diverse peoples so recently escaped from the Keeper's cage, there was no trace. Then, as the cavern grew darker yet and the pace of its disintegration accelerated, he raced the clock across the desert and out into the nighted places of deeper dream . . .

Later, high over the Southern Sea and under a sky that was beginning to fill with evening, as they sped for Ulthar and the haven that the City of Cats offered, de Marigny thought to ask of Crow: 'What was it, that place?'

Tiania answered him. 'It was one of those places where Cthulhu manufactures nightmares with which to terrorize dreaming mortals.'

Crow nodded. 'Yes, and there must be a number of places like it in dreamland. Factories where Cthulhu employs the Machineries of Horror to amplify his loathsome dreams before transmitting them to the minds of sensitive dreamers. Tiania and I almost became the raw

155

materials such factories consume. Yes, we were very nearly part of it, Henri. *Aegri somnia vana!'*

'"Dreams of a diseased mind,"' de Marigny translated with an involuntary shudder. 'Ah, well – that's one factory I wasn't sorry to close down, Titus. No, not at all.'

Part Five

1

Ilek-Vad

After three days of somewhat crowded but contented recuperation at the home of Grant Enderby in Ulthar – three days of almost complete peace and quiet, marred only by the knowledge that soon they must once more be about the task in hand – Titus Crow, Henri-Laurent de Marigny, and Tiania of Elysia convened at the Inn of a Thousand Sleeping Cats, taking a secluded table in an alcove where they could talk in utmost privacy.

They were dressed now in rich robes of dream's styling. Tiania wore a low-cut flowing gown of mother-of-pearl whose mobile, greenly glowing tints matched her hair perfectly; Crow sported a short jacket of yellow silk, with matching Eastern-styled trousers supported by a wide black belt; de Marigny had chosen a single-piece suit of scarlet satin, throwing his black flying cloak carelessly about his shoulders. In their cool alcove they relaxed, toyed with their food, which at the Inn of a Thousand Sleeping Cats is the best in all dreamland, and sipped exotic liqueurs.

Eventually, almost reluctantly, Titus Crow opened the conversation. 'Now, Henri, how did you get on at the temple of the Elder Ones yesterday evening? Was Atal able to offer any more help?'

'Well,' de Marigny began, 'first of all I told him how well things had worked out: about our escape from Dylath-Leen, the destruction of the great ruby and the Fly-the-Light, the death of the Keeper and his – pets – and more or less everything else that happened in between. He was particularly pleased that his elixir had served me so well.

'Then I told him how we planned to go Ilek-Vad . . .' He paused and shrugged. 'I'm afraid I drew something of a blank there, Titus. Atal could only repeat what Kthanid told me in the Hall of Crystal and Pearl: that there is some sort of screen about Ilek-Vad, one that lets nothing in or out.'

'Drawn a blank, eh?' Crow repeated after a while. 'Maybe, and maybe not. I'm inclined to look on the bright side. Look at it this way: a screen has two sides, Henri. True, it might have been built, this screen, by enemies of dreamland, to keep people from knowing what was going on in there. But on the other hand, might it not have been built to keep Cthulhu's invasion forces out?'

'You think that perhaps Randolph Carter and my father –'

'That they built this screen? I think it's possible. As to what they're doing behind it, in Ilek-Vad, that's another matter. It's something we'll have to find out for ourselves. And there's really only one way to do that.'

'We're going to Ilek-Vad!' Tiania put in, excitement in her beautiful voice.

'No,' said Crow, 'not you, Tiania. Henri and I – *we* are going to Ilek-Vad.'

'Titus,' she answered, 'I'm not letting you out of my sight again, not for a moment. There are too many terrors in this dreamland of yours. What would I do if any harm befell you?'

'And what would I do if harm befell you, Tiania? No, you stay here in Ulthar, at Grant Enderby's house. I'll know you're safe there. It will only be for a day or two, until we know what's going on, then we'll be back. And don't argue. You might be able to sway Kthanid, but not me.'

Tiania pursed her lips and sat back, eyes flashing angrily. De Marigny coughed and hastily asked: 'When do we set out?' He was already beginning to feel his stomach tighten as the Unknown loomed once more before him.

'Tomorrow morning, at dawn,' Crow answered. 'We're known to be here in dreamland now, so it's useless to attempt any sort of stealth. We leave at first light, in the time-clock.'

'Then you two will have to excuse me,' said de Marigny, rising to his feet.

'Oh? An early night, Henri?' Crow asked.

'No, I'm meeting with . . . someone.'

'I have seen the way she looks at you!' Tiania laughed mischievously, her disappointment already forgotten.

'She?' Crow frowned. Then his face brightened. 'Oh, you mean Litha, Grant Enderby's daughter.' He too laughed, then warned: 'But remember, Henri, that beautiful as she is with those huge dark eyes of hers, she's only a dream.'

'I'll endorse that heartily,' de Marigny answered, turning away to hide the sudden flush that suffused his face. 'She is a dream, isn't she?'

And so Titus Crow and Henri-Laurent de Marigny set out at dawn's first light, leaving Tiania behind at the friendly house of Grant Enderby in Ulthar. And by midday they were well out over the twilight sea.

They could have traveled at a greater speed, certainly, but Crow was fascinated by the topography of dreamland. He had closely scanned all of the rivers, towns, lakes, islands, and villages as they passed in endless procession beneath the time-clock. Now he silently appreciated the calm, peaceful, scintillating surface of the twilight sea.

For the twilight sea is a vast inland ocean (whose name derives from a perpetual serenity reminiscent of that of lonely lakes on calm summer evenings) far to the west of dreamland's third greatest continent. There, on a high promontory of volcanic glass that reaches far out over blue waters, stands Ilek-Vad – city of fabulous towers, domes, and turrets – once seat of a proud line of ancient kings, palace-city now of King Carter, late of the waking world.

Below the time-clock as it sped high over the wavelets, Crow and de Marigny could make out the coral-like labyrinths of the bearded and finny Gnorri, industrious dwellers in crystal depths. And it was as they scanned the marvelous intricacy of the Gnorri's incessant subaqueous labors, while yet Ilek-Vad lay a good ten miles distant, that the time-clock suddenly began to act very strangely indeed. Refusing to obey Crow's commands, the vessel veered to one side and began to fly in a wide circle which would eventually carry it *around* Ilek-Vad but no *closer* to that splendid city.

After a minute or so of wrestling with the clock's mind-controls, Crow grunted: 'Huh! Well, there's your screen, Henri, and a damned effective one at that!'

'That's amazing!' de Marigny replied. 'It must be similar to the Wall of Naach-Tith that Grant Enderby told me about. An invisible, impenetrable wall. A force-screen. But how . . .?'

'Science, Henri – or sorcery. Remember that this is Earth's dreamland, and men have been dreaming of such devices for a long, long time. In any case, what does it matter? The wall exists, and we're on the wrong side of it.'

'Do you suppose,' asked de Marigny, thoughtfully, 'that the barrier goes down under the twilight sea?'

'We can soon find out,' Crow answered, and he caused the time-clock to dive down, down into blue waters where the Gnorri swam and ogled and constructed their calcium caves and labyrinths. And there they once more came up against the invisible wall. But here there was a strange thing: the Gnorri were unobstructed in their submarine activities! For them the barrier did not exist, and they swam without hindrance to and fro across the invisible line.

'Well, now,' Crow mused. 'And I wonder how the birds fare?'

Up he took the clock and out of the calm waters with barely a splash. And there in the sky they waited until a cloud of white birds like geese, with a harsh, surprised gabble of inquiry, parted to fly around the clock and on through the invisible barrier.

'And the clouds themselves,' said de Marigny, watching in the scanners the passage of fleecy clouds into regions where the clock was forbidden. 'I don't understand . . .'

'I think I do,' Crow said. 'The Gnorri, the birds and clouds, they are all, well, *natural* things. They are the harmless, everyday, commonplace realities of dreamland, with no special allegiances to any powers, good or evil. The clock, on the other hand – yes, and its passengers – we are the aliens here.'

'But Atal, and Kthanid before him, said that *nothing* could get in or out of Ilek-Vad,' de Marigny protested.

Crow shrugged. 'What would they know about birds or clouds or the Gnorri, Henri? No, Ilek-Vad is only forbidden to alien things and to things which would fathom her secrets. Forbidden to alien scanners on alien worlds, and to alien Elder Gods that use such scanners. Forbidden to the shew-stones of dreamland's magicians – black or white – because shew-stones are not natural but supernatural, alien. Forbidden to the minions of the CCD, and to Nyarlathotep, *Their* messenger and agent.'

'And to us,' de Marigny added, 'because of the clock, no doubt. A device of the Elder Gods and alien to dreamland.'

'Oh, the clock is alien, all right,' Crow nodded, a stubborn frown wrinkling his forehead. 'It's damned ingenious, too. I don't think this barrier will stop us for too long, Henri.'

'Titus, I don't see –'

'Listen, my friend. In this clock I've escaped from the awesome pull of a black hole in space, an omnivorous freak of nature from which not even light may flee. I did it not by going around the black hole but simply by moving . . . *away* from it! You see, the clock isn't only a space-time machine but a gateway between intermediary dimensions, too. The proof of that statement lies in the simple fact that the clock is here in dreamland right now, in that you yourself have used it to travel between dimensions, Henri. For dreamland after all is only a parallel dimension existing on a level compatible to the subconscious mind of man.

'But I didn't only escape from a black hole; I've also been safely into and out of the prison dimension of Yog-Sothoth, the Lurker at the Threshold, where not even one of Kthanid's Great Thoughts could follow. Yes, and from there into Elysia itself! Why, the clock slips between dimensions as easily as it flies through space and time!' He paused. 'But there, we've wasted enough of the latter, now let's see just how resourceful the time-clock really is.'

In the space of the next ten minutes Titus Crow piloted the clock into as many again parallel dimensions, using the semisentient machine in a way which might baffle even the Elder Gods themselves. De Marigny was astounded at the view the scanners gave him of these remarkable planes of existence. Some of them seemed darkly-gaseous, nighted places, where vague shadowy shapes moved inexplicably; others were riots of primal color, to the apparent exclusion of all else. In two more there were definite geometric shapes, but Crow was quick to leave the latter planes; he was leery of the interest certain sharply-angled shapes displayed in the time-clock.

What most surprised de Marigny, however, was the fact that in several of these parallel universes the barrier about

Ilek-Vad – or rather, the barriers about corresponding areas in the alien spaces and times – was not only extant but visible. In one it showed in the scanners as a vast, silvery shimmering sphere, in another as an opaque pyramid of enormous proportions. But in all its various manifestations one thing about the barrier remained constant: to the time-clock it was impenetrable.

Then, as Crow switched dimensions yet again – to emerge in a scarlet glare through which thin bars of green light appeared to shoot in every conceivable direction without ever colliding – he gave a cry of triumph. 'This is it, Henri, our gateway into Ilek-Vad. The barrier doesn't extend into this subdimension, the scanners show no trace of it. We simply move forward, in a physical sense, like this –' The alien universe outside the clock seemed momentarily to whirl. 'And then we slide back through the intermediate dimensions to dreamland!'

There followed a kaleidoscopic confusion of weird colors, shapes, and motions as Crow returned the time-clock sideways through a dozen intervening planes of existence; and at last they emerged again above the twilight sea. All was as it had been, except that now they were moving forward, toward Ilek-Vad, and they were at last within the ten-mile boundary line of the invisible force-screen.

And there ahead and below was Ilek-Vad itself, fabulous city of towers, turrets, and domes rising up from the hollow glass cliffs wherein its foundations are housed, straddling the volcanic promontory beneath whose heights the Gnorri labor ceaselessly in the twilight sea. The afternoon sun shone down on Ilek-Vad, reflecting brilliantly from windows and bright metal statues, and in the city's squares and gardens brightly garbed crowds gathered to watch the approach of the weird aerial visitor.

As they drew even closer to the city, de Marigny's attention was drawn to what looked like a huge mirror at the very tip of the glassy promontory. At the base of this device, at what looked like a control bank, a pair of helmeted – soldiers? – busied themselves. Then, all around the rim of the city, many apertures appeared simultaneously in rampart walls, and out from these openings trundled more of the great mirrors.

'Titus,' de Marigny began, 'I don't think I quite like –' But before he could finish, suddenly Ilek-Vad seemed to disintegrate in a blinding flash of light that bloomed outward from the great mirrors. Actually the city had suffered no harm whatever, and as quickly as it had come the blinding glare died down – only to repeat a moment later as once more the vast mirrors hurled forth their incredibly bright beams of light.

The answer was now obvious, and Crow gave voice to de Marigny's unspoken thought:

'Those things are weapons, Henri!' he cried. 'And damn it, *they're firing them at us!*'

2

Warlords of Dream

Half-a-dozen times at least the clock was caught in a crisscross of blinding rays from the projector-batteries about the city, before an astonished Titus Crow even thought to make a move to avoid them. By then such a move would have been superfluous; it was obvious that the beams of dazzling white light were neither damaging nor impeding the clock.

The troops manning the projectors saw this too, and moments later a second screen – this time a flickering, redly coruscating dome of purely physical energies – went up to enclose the city proper.

'No good, my friends,' Crow grinned. 'That's not going to keep us out either.' He flew the time-clock forward and, as if the redly flickering screen did not exist at all, the vehicle of the Elder Gods passed through the curtain of energies without pause.

Into the heart of the city Titus Crow flew the clock, slowly and carefully now, not wishing to alarm Ilek-Vad's inhabitants more than was absolutely unavoidable. Finally, after hanging motionless for a few seconds over the gardens of the central palace itself, he set the clock down between tinkling fountains and exotic flowering shrubs.

Shortly thereafter a thousand soldiers, attired in lightly armored suits with shining metal helmets, emerged from new, barrack-like buildings in the outer gardens to surround the time-clock and take up defensive positions. They wore swords and carried shields which bore in their centers small versions of the mirror-like ray projectors.

None of these troops came any closer to the time-clock than thirty or forty feet, and once they were in position behind their shields they made no further threatening move. Crow and de Marigny were content for the moment to remain in the complete safety of their vehicle and await developments – which were not long in coming.

Escorted by some two-dozen personal guardsmen, approaching on foot and dressed in splendidly opulent robes of silver and gold cloth, a strange, slender personage came from the direction of the palace itself. The soldiers around him were patently men of Ilek-Vad, and they had obviously been selected for their task. But while they were noticeably taller than the average inhabitants of dreamland, nevertheless the man they protected stood head and shoulders taller than the tallest of them.

'That man,' said de Marigny. 'He's as tall as I am. Is he young or . . . old? I can't quite make up my mind. And surely he's –'

'A man from the waking world?' Crow asked it for him; and answered: 'Yes, he is, Henri. And unless I'm very much mistaken, we're singularly honored. Oh, yes, see? He recognizes the time-clock! And so he should, for he used it long before I even knew it existed.'

'Randolph Carter!' De Marigny nodded his acknowledgment, awed in spite of himself. 'King Carter of Ilek-Vad!'

Now the king waved his guardsmen back and came right up to the clock. His face was pale, slender, that of a young gentleman, but his shoulder-length hair was white and his eyes old with incredible wisdom. Amazement shone in those eyes now and, as Titus Crow had noted, recognition. He reached out his hands and touched the clock, saying:

'Whoever you are, please come out now. I know that you mean no harm, for if you did, then by now my city would be falling around me. You have my word that no harm will come to you in Ilek-Vad. See, I know your vehicle well . . .'

As King Carter's hands moved expertly along the clock's sides there came an odd clicking from some hidden mechanism. The tall man stepped nimbly back as the clock's front panel swung silently open beneath the weird, four-handed dial, and his eyes scrutinized the clock's passengers minutely as they emerged.

Then, plainly perplexed at some as yet unknown thing, after taking Crow's hand in a somewhat cursory greeting he grasped de Marigny's shoulders and stared hard at him. The frown deepened then on his own face and he shook his head in mystification.

'For a moment I thought that . . . you look so very much like . . . someone.'

'I know who you are,' answered the object of the king's scrutiny, 'but I'm pretty sure we never met – or if we did I was only a very small child at the time. I am Henri-Laurent de Marigny, and this is Titus Crow.'

Now the king's lantern jaw fell open in an unashamed gasp of astonishment. His grip tightened on the other's shoulders. 'Then you *are* a de Marigny! By all the lands of dream, I should have guessed it! Who could possibly look more like his father than a son? Only a twin, I think, and believe me you *are* the twin of Etienne as he was . . . how long ago?

'But this is unforgivable of me. I have guests from the waking world – the son of my trusted friend and counselor, Etienne-Laurent de Marigny, and your friend here, Mr. Crow – and here we stand chatting in the garden! Forgive me, forgive me, and come with me please to the palace. There is much to talk about. I don't know why you're here, but I feel it's a good omen – and by the Sign of Koth, dreamland needs all the good omens she can get!'

* * *

'So,' said the king much later, after they had dined and when he knew all about his visitors – from their initial encounters with the CCD, through Titus Crow's venturings in space and time and de Marigny's attempt to find Elysia for himself, right up to the present moment – 'then I was right. It was an omen, your coming here. You could have chosen no more opportune time, for at this very moment we prepare for war against dream's minions of the CCD, against the nightmares of the Great Old Ones themselves.

'In you two we have powerful allies, and already you have struck telling blows against the evil in dreamland. Yes, great allies indeed! Why, you, Titus Crow, have seen Elysia, and for all my wanderings I never found my way there!'

'But your name is known there,' Crow answered, equally gallant. 'And as for encounters with the CCD: what other man has sought out, even confronted Nyarlathotep? And escaped sane!'

'That was long ago,' the king modestly answered, 'and I was by no means as great a dreamer as the stories have it. No, my adventures in dreamland were often ill-advised. I was lucky, believe me. Nyarlathotep will not let me go so lightly next time.'

'And you think there may be a next time?' de Marigny asked.

'It seems more than possible,' King Carter nodded. 'There are warlords stalking dreamland even now, and war itself cannot be far behind.'

'Warlords?' Crow questioned.

'Myself and Kuranes, yes, and others, too. And then, of course, there are also our enemies, the warlords of the CCD! Of the latter you know as much, possibly more than I do.' He paused for a moment of contemplation, then went on:

'Like myself, Kuranes trains his generals; and in the

sky-islands about cloud-floating Serannian he builds a great armada of sky-yachts and yearns for the day when he may once more return to the throne in timeless Celephais. Until that day Celephais remains behind its own force-screen, safe for now from the CCD, dreaming more wondrously than any other city in all dreamland.'

The king laughed wryly before continuing. 'Strange, I was hardly a warlike man in the waking world, but I shall command armies in dreamland! Mind you, it will not be the first time I have commanded the legions of dream, but those were strange dreams indeed.' He paused again. 'However – I would like you two to assist me, to be my generals. Certainly you know more of such matters than I, as your very presence here testifies. To have fought so long and hard against Cthulhu's hideous brethren – and to survive the unending battle! I fear, though, that new phases of that eternal conflict are in the offing.'

'Sir,' said Crow, 'we would gladly join you, but there are many things we should like to know. Neither one of us is a great dreamer, and –'

'I understand,' King Carter nodded, 'but do not underestimate your ability to dream, my friends. Dreams are all things to all men, and men must shape their own dreams just as they shape their destinies in the waking world. Now, what is it you wish to know?'

'I want to know about my father,' de Marigny immediately answered. 'While we dined you mentioned his absence. If he is not here in Ilek-Vad, where is he?'

The king smiled. 'Ah, Etienne. Where is he, you ask? Where indeed? He set out some years ago, before this latest trouble in dreamland began. His destination? Who can say? Let me explain that Etienne has become the greatest of all human dreamers. His dream-quests are unending; they have carried him beyond hitherto undreamed of regions – not only in Earth's dreamlands

171

but in those of distant worlds and dimensions.

'He will return – of course he will – but I cannot say when. There was a period of peace in dreamland when he left, but it did not last. I would have gone with him . . .' he shrugged, 'except that my adopted people are here in Ilek-Vad. So, at the moment I am both king and counselor. But make no mistake, Henri, your father will return. Someday . . .

'However, if you would be satisfied merely to see his *physical* form – why, that is simple! Come –'

The king led the way to one of the palace's inner sanctums where, upon a marble divan covered with rich silks and soft cushions, reclined the motionless form of Etienne-Laurent de Marigny. Wan and breathless, seemingly frozen in death, but undecayed, the spirit merely – absent – for the moment.

'He –' de Marigny broke the hush, 'he is as I remember him. And this trancelike state of his: you and Tiania share this same type of sleep, Titus. You looked so much like this when I saw you in Elysia.'

'Don't disturb yourself, Henri,' Crow quietly said, sensing the depth of his friend's emotion. 'It's simply a very deep form of dreaming. Worlds without end at his fingertips, my friend, and your father one of the greatest seekers of all time. Who knows what wonders he may be seeing even now? Would you really call him back?'

De Marigny made no attempt to answer.

For a long while the three men stood looking at the silent figure on the divan.

3

The Curse of Cthulhu

The next morning after breakfast King Carter of Ilek-Vad
set out to tell his visitors of the shadow over Earth's
dreamland, the curse of Cthulhu. Since Crow and de
Marigny were aware of the general threat, the king con-
fined himself to specific areas of the peril. He explained
the defenses which he and Kuranes and several others
had set up before it, detailing the forces they intended
to throw against it.

The threat itself was of course the insidious encroach-
ment of Cthulhu's minions into dreamland, bringing His
Word with them and spreading horror and evil wherever
they were permitted to infiltrate men's dreams. If they
were not stopped, eventually dreamland would be simply
a barren place of nightmare and abomination, and the
dreams of men would belong to Cthulhu to do with
them as he desired. Following that, of course, the Lord
of R'lyeh's next step would be an invasion of the waking
world itself, the control of the conscious as well as the
subconscious minds of men.

Against this threat – which King Carter himself had
warned of long ago while yet an inexperienced wanderer
in dreamland, though even he had not realized how far
the cancer might spread – certain barriers had already
been raised, behind which preparations had forged ahead
to thwart, even repel the creeping invasion. Of these
barriers two were believed to be completely impassable
to anything tainted by the curse of Cthulhu: the force-
screens about Celephais and Ilek-Vad. But even so, the
inhabitants of those cities took no chances, for they were

sworn to defy this persecution by Cthulhu's alien dreams. Hence the ray-projectors with which the Ilek-Vadians had bombarded the time-clock.

And behind the force-screens the armies of dreamland were being trained and its armadas built, strange weapons devised and plans for great battles laid. The King of Ilek-Vad had five thousand soldiers who would fight for him to the death, and in cloud-floating Cerannian Kuranes had built fifty great sky-yachts and was presently building fifty more.

Even before the arrival of Crow and de Marigny plans had been laid for an assault on Dylath-Leen. The intention was to rid the city forever of the horned ones of Leng, then to hold and protect its boundaries. Eventually the place might once more support the honest folk of dreamland, who would then patrol and protect the city's boundaries themselves.

Thus would Dylath-Leen become an outpost against the horned invaders, who would receive short shrift if ever they dared sail their abhorrent vessels into its harbors again. With the glad news that Carter's visitors brought, however – that the power of the horned ones in Dylath-Leen was destroyed, however temporarily, and that in all likelihood they had already fled the city in their great black galleys – now it would be only a matter of days before the first of Kuranes' anti-gravity boats with its complement of Ilek-Vadian soldier-crewmen departed for Dylath-Leen.

Nor would the reclamation of dreamland's cities, those fallen into evil ways, end with Dylath-Leen. There were other suspect places lying far to the west, along the coast of the great Southern Sea. Zak, for instance, with its terraced temples wherein forgotten dreams fade and slowly vanish, seldom to be resurrected, would be an ideal haunt for Cthulhu's emissaries: there they might experience all the dreams of Man's youth, and thereby perhaps determine the course of dreams yet to come.

174

Then there was infamous Thalarion, the Demon City of a Thousand Dark Wonders, reigned over by the eidolon Lathi whose fleshly avatar was rumored to be of the Cthulhu Cycle Deities themselves! Surely, in a place where images of the CCD had been openly, immemorially worshipped, there would be many unwholesome things to root out and destroy. And what of the Charnel Gardens of Zura, land of pleasures unattained; and Sona-Nyl, a region of fancy where, legend had it, future dreams were shaped and implanted like seeds in the receptive minds of certain waking men, there to blossom and grow into full-fledged dreams in their own right? What a marvelous coup *that* would be for Cthulhu's minions!

As to how the friends and enemies of dreamland might be recognized one from the other, King Carter said that the true men of dreamland were dreamland's true friends, of whom only a handful were under Cthulhu's evil spell. The horned ones of Leng were not true men – indeed, they could hardly be said to be men at all – but were of the dreamland of a dark dimension paralleling Yuggoth on the Rim, whence the CCD had brought them when the dreams of men were very young.

And apart from true men and pseudo-men there were also the utterly inhuman creatures of dream, some sentient and others barely so. The loyalty of these beings was more often than not highly suspect. The 'G' creatures, for instance, were especially suspicious – the gugs, ghasts and ghouls – and only slightly less sinister were the others: the shantaks, dholes and zoogs.

King Carter had had much to do with all such creatures in his youth, and in some of them he had found very strange allies indeed. The cats of Ulthar all knew and loved him; the zoogs of the Enchanted Wood were not disinclined toward him. He had even befriended the ghouls of dreamland's nether-pits, whose leader was a special acquaintance of his.

As to the ghasts and gugs, mercifully they were usually content to remain in their own realms. The ghasts were least bothersome in that real light destroyed them. They were rarely to be found outside the lightless Vaults of Zin, where they were hunted by and in turn hunted the gigantic gugs.

Night-gaunts, however, were not to be dealt with so lightly. Though faceless, they were nevertheless believed to be the secret eyes of Cthulhu's minions in dreamland. Moreover, many of dream's people still believed that the night-gaunts held great power over all of dream's lesser creatures. And certainly the vast and hippocephalic shantak-birds were mortally afraid of them. Chiefly to be found near the summit of Ngranek on the Isle of Oriab, night-gaunts also guarded the grim gray peaks dividing Leng and Inquanok, where they spent the drab daylight hours in caves that scarred the topmost pinnacles. In the night, though, gaunts flew far and wide throughout dreamland, and their secretive nature was such that indeed they would make ideal spies for the CCD.

One of the first tasks for Kuranes' sky-yachts, once Dylath-Leen was secured, would be to destroy the night-gaunt stronghold atop Ngranek, then to block all of those entrances leading down into the black and reeking abyss beneath. In this manner that area of the underworld and all its terrors would be shut off forever from saner, upper regions of dream.

And so the armies of dream would go from strength to strength. Eventually there would be great battle-fleets upon the Southern Sea, barring access to the black galleys of the horned ones; vast stone fortresses would be built and manned along the border of Inquanok and Leng, ensuring that the horrors of the latter tableland might forever remain remote. Finally, a way would be sought to destroy those black places in dreamland – the evil foci of CCD influence – where Cthulhu's engines of nightmare

176

pounded detestably, poisoning the healthy dreams of Earth's mortals.

Such places were known to exist in the Enchanted Wood, in certain green deeps of the Southern Sea, even in the perfumed and often beautiful jungles of fabled Kled; others were rumored to lie in subterranean vaults beneath Zura's elusive temples, and in the hinterland of ruined, primordial Sarkomand. There were many, many places to be freed or cleansed of the curse of Cthulhu; great battles to be fought and won; temples of evil to be razed and healthy frontier cities founded. And all to free Man's subconscious mind from the canker of CCD-inspired nightmares.

For unless Cthulhu's creeping incursion into dreams could be put an end to, neither the waking world of men nor the universe itself would ever be truly safe from the horror inherent in His aeon-devised design for the utter destruction of all sanity and order.

Such were the grim and doom-fraught subjects covered by King Carter through all of that long day; but in the evening a banquet was prepared in honor of the visitors from the waking world, and as they sipped the clean red wine of Ilek-Vad so their apprehension for dreamland's future eased a little. Later, reclining in silk-cushioned couches that swung gently to and fro beneath the crystal-clear dome of the city's highest tower, gazing out across the placid twilight sea where all the stars of night gleamed in a darkly fluid firmament, Crow and de Marigny talked a while and then fell silent. Both of them were thinking the same thing: they knew now all they had wanted to know of Ilek-Vad. It was time to move on.

The next morning King Carter wrote a letter of introduction for his visitors, a warrant authorizing their new ranks as Generals of the Armies of Dream, telling briefly of their origins and their present importance to all dreamland.

They were to take this letter with them to Kuranes in cloud-floating Serannian, the pink marble city of the clouds; for the pair had intimated their desire to be once more on their way, and Serannian was to be their next stop.

Thus, at noon of that same day, the dreamers said their farewells to the king and flew up in the time-clock over the city. And as the powers that sustained the great invisible dome of hyperdimensional energy were momentarily revoked by Ilek-Vad's wizards, they sped away over the twilight sea in the direction of Serannian.

'Titus,' said de Marigny as they gained speed, 'things seem to be working out very well.'

'At the moment, yes. Does it bother you?'

'Something bothers me. But it's difficult to pin it down. I mean, everything seems so easy now – the obstacles are behind us.'

'Perhaps they are.'

'And yet I somehow feel an urgency, a need for greater haste.'

Crow nodded. 'I feel it too. My instinct tells me that all is not as well as it might be.'

'And there are still many questions,' de Marigny went on. 'For instance, the weapons we've seen so far. Are they magical or mechanical?'

'A bit of both, I suspect. But that takes us back to an old argument, Henri: just what *is* magic? This is Earth's dreamland, remember? If you had been to Elysia with me, then you might finally be able to put that word "magic" behind you. In Elysia there are islands that float a mile in the air, just like Serannian. Surely the science that holds such islands aloft is little short of "magical"? What you must remember is this: whether in the waking world or the world of dream, if man wants something badly enough to be, he will *make it be!* Is a sky-yacht any more fantastic than an airplane? Are King Carter's ray-projectors any stranger than lasers? Dreamland and the waking world are two different spheres, Henri, certainly – but both were shaped in the minds of men, sleeping and waking alike!'

De Marigny frowned, then suddenly burst out: 'Star-stones! That's something else that's been bothering me – are there no star-stones in dreamland? I had one hanging from a chain around my neck when I set out from Earth, but I'm damned if it's there now!'

'Ah!' Crow smiled. 'But the star-stones came to Earth from an alien universe, Henri, an alien dimension. Dreamland guards her boundaries well; she does not gladly suffer that which is not of Earth and Man's own dreaming.'

'But what of Cthulhu and the CCD?' de Marigny argued. 'What could possibly be more alien? And yet their emissaries are here.'

'Sentience!' Crow answered. 'They are here because Cthulhu wills it, just as we are here because we will it.' He shrugged. 'Quite apart from which, of course, Cthulhu is a master of dreams. And it could be argued, too, that we are the aliens on Earth and not the CCD. After all, they were here first – millions of years before man. Perhaps Cthulhu himself has put this stricture on the star-stones of ancient Mnar, that they may not exist in dreams. It has certainly taken us long enough to remember them and question their absence.'

'Hmph!' de Marigny grunted. 'It's very odd: one minute everything seems so easy, the next – impossible!'

'That's the way of it, Henri,' Crow agreed. 'Often things are far simpler in dreams – but then again they can be a damned sight more difficult, too.'

4

Serannian

At first sight, even knowing he was dreaming, de Marigny found Serannian almost unbelievable. He had seen it before, certainly, in those telepathic visions showed to him by Kthanid in hyperdimensional Elysia, but the reality was a far greater thing. A cloud-washed coast of pink marble that seemed to stretch away to its own horizons; and built upon the shore, a splendid city that looked out over an ethereal sea of glowing cirrus and cirrocumulus.

Far below, glimpsed through roseate mists and pink-hued clouds, the Cerenarian Sea's white-tipped billows washed towards a distance-hazed land where Mount Aran was only just visible. That mountain, the dreamers knew, formed one of the valley-walls of Ooth-Nargai, where timeless Celephais reared her splendid domes, towers, and minarets beneath a dome of energy like that which protected Ilek-Vad. But because Celephais and Serannian both came under Kuranes' wise rule, trade went on as of old between the Timeless City and the Sky Islands; except that now the force-screen about the former must periodically be relaxed, allowing the sky-galleys that brought the latter's supplies free passage out onto the Cerenarian Sea.

Indeed, the galleys they saw riding to the horizon, where they sailed skyward on rose-tinted mists, had recently put out from Celephais. Awed by the beauty of all they saw – marveling that the subconscious mind of man could dream such wonders – the travelers in the time-clock followed one of the galleys into the harbor of Serannian; and when

Crow set the clock down on the walls of the pink-marble docks, they marveled again that Serannian had ever been built here, on this ethereal coast where the west wind flowed into the sky.

Moored in the harbor, floating impossibly on pink cloud-crests, the dreamers spied twenty-five of Kuranes' fleet of fifty war vessels; along their decks, port and starboard, were single rows of mirror-bright devices that reflected sharp shafts of sunlight as the ships bobbed up and down. These were ray-projectors, like those they had seen in Ilek-Vad. In the distant sky, riding out on the west wind, the other half of the fleet was under sail.

Standing beside the time-clock on the dockside – which was deserted now, for sailors and dockers alike had quietly melted away into the wharfside taverns as soon as the time-clock had landed – Crow and de Marigny watched the receding sails of the ships until a voice informed: 'They go out to practice the arts of war, arts which will soon be put to good use in Dylath-Leen and other places.'

Turning, they came face to face with Kuranes, a man once of the waking world, now Lord of Ooth-Nargai, Celephais, and the Sky around Serannian. They knew him immediately from a description furnished by King Carter. Slightly built but regally robed, gray-bearded but sprightly and bright-eyed – and wary – Kuranes had with him a retinue of pike-armed guardsmen. He gazed briefly upon his visitors before continuing.

'Rumors have been reaching me for days now of a strange flying machine come into Earth's dreamland.' He made a motion with his hand and the guardsmen clustered closer, moving between the two dreamers and their machine. Crow and de Marigny found themselves inside a circle of sharp pikeheads.

'I have wondered,' Kuranes went on, 'whether this device, this flying machine, was benign toward dreamland

181

or – malignant.' Again he beckoned, and his guardsmen laid restraining hands on the two strangers.

At last Crow spoke. 'Lord Kuranes, we understand your apprehension perfectly, but you may put your mind at ease simply by reading this letter.' He produced the carefully folded document. 'It is from Randolph Carter in Ilek-Vad.'

'A letter from Randolph Carter?' Kuranes' eyebrows went up and he seemed surprised. 'Randolph, you say? Are you so familiar, then, with the King of Ilek-Vad?'

'My father was King Carter's counselor,' de Marigny quickly answered, 'before he took to exploring in undreamed of places. I am Henri-Laurent de Marigny, and this is Titus Crow.'

As Kuranes read King Carter's letter, so the attitude of alert wariness fell from him. Finally he smiled and waved his guardsmen aside, clasping first de Marigny's hand, then Titus Crow's.

'Gentlemen,' he said, 'I am at your service.'

A few minutes later, on their way to Kuranes' 'palace' – which, astonishingly, they saw at a distance to be nothing less than a great Gothic manorhouse with a gray stone tower, typical of lordly English dwellings Kuranes had known in the Cornwall of his youth in the waking world – a servant of the Lord of Serannian approached in great haste. This man, a whiskered butler attired in typically English livery, though patently he was a denizen of dreamland, probably born and bred in Celephais or Ulthar, handed Kuranes a tiny metal tube.

Kuranes took square-framed spectacles from his robe and put them on, then unscrewed one end of the metal tube and carefully extracted a tightly rolled strip of extremely thin paper. 'James,' he asked of his butler, 'what color was the bird that delivered this?'

'Pink as Serannian's clouds, my Lord,' the butler answered, in an accent which was not quite Cornish.

'Hmm . . . Then it came from Atal in Ulthar. I wonder what he wants.'

On hearing Atal's name spoken, the two dreamers exchanged quick, speculative glances. Then de Marigny's suddenly taut features relaxed and he shrugged, murmuring: 'It can have nothing to do with us, Titus. No one knows we're here.'

'Oh?' exclaimed Kuranes, his sharp ears catching de Marigny's remark. 'But you are wrong, my young friend! It does concern you – both of you. And as to how Atal knew you would be here – none in dreamland is wise as Atal. Did he know you were going to Ilek-Vad?'

The two nodded in unison.

'Then it would not be hard to guess your next port of call.' His eyes went back to the paper. 'It says that you should return to Ulthar at once, that many of Leng's horned ones are in the city disguised as foreign traders, and that a man called Grant Enderby is worried about strange figures seen lurking near his house in the dead of night.'

'Anything else?' Crow's voice was tense.

'Yes. Atal says that although there are no true soldiers in Ulthar – that is, no real force for the protection of the public – he has sent several young priests from the Temple of the Elder Ones to keep a discreet watch over Enderby's house. Hmm! And that's all there is. It seems to have been penned in some haste.'

He handed the letter to Crow. 'Take it, by all means, but you'll have to take my word for what's in it. It's written in an obscure glyph with which only a few in dreamland are familiar. Atal knows that I am one of the few.'

'Lord Kuranes,' said de Marigny, his voice urgent, 'you must understand, we have loved ones in Ulthar. It's more than possible that our mutual enemies intend them harm.'

'Yes,' Crow continued when de Marigny paused. 'It seems we must take our leave of you sooner than we expected. Immediately.'

Kuranes nodded. 'I understand. It's a pity, for I was looking forward to a long talk. It's rare now that I have distinguished visitors from the waking world. You will go in your flying machine, of course?'

'Yes,' Crow answered, 'but as soon as we get another chance we'll be back to try your hospitality, Kuranes.'

'You won't find it wanting,' the Lord of Serannian promised. 'But listen, I have an idea. This could be my chance to exercise my armada a bit more realistically. It's known that the horned ones have a number of sky-galleys of their own. In fact, they once kidnapped King Carter to dreamland's moon – which is not like the moon of the waking world – in just such a galley. This could be how they plan to make their getaway from Ulthar once their dirty work, whatever it is, is done there. It's not unlikely that they've hidden one of their foul galleys somewhere on the coast, to which they'll flee when they're ready. How would it be if I sent a dozen of my sky-yachts, with full complement of trained crew-men, to follow you to Ulthar?'

'It's a very kind offer,' Crow answered, 'but the time-clock travels at an incredible pace. We'd leave your ships far behind. Still, I think it would be a good idea to send some of your vessels to Ulthar, perhaps to station them there permanently. There have always been a few horned ones in the city, or so I'm led to believe, and we can never tell what nests they may have built for themselves. Why not let a handful of your best ships and their crews form the city's first soldiery, a police force to guard against the subversion of the horned ones?'

'I'll do it!' Kuranes cried. 'Even if my ships can be of no assistance to you two, still they can perform a useful service for the peoples of Ulthar. In any case, I can only send a handful of ships, for I'm short of crews. I'm to draw upon Ilek-Vad for most of my crewmen. Now then, I can see that you're eager to be off, so I won't hold you. Off you go – and the very best of British luck to you!' He waved after them as they turned and hurriedly retraced their steps in the direction of the harbor.

To the young priest who anxiously scanned the skies from the roof of the temple's ivied tower, the coming of the clock into Ulthar was an awe-inspiring experience. Having seen many marvels as an initiate and acolyte at the Temple of the Elder Ones, he was used to wonders, but this was somehow different. There was no clap of thunder, no darkening over of the skies, none of the phenomena with which he was used to associating the onset of occult or paranormal occurrences. And yet surely this flying clock was a magick of the first water.

Out of an early afternoon sky touched with fleece the time-clock raced – at first a dot spied among the distant clouds, then a dark oblong shape that flew upright, finally a coffin shape that slowed and fell out of the sky – down past the tower so that the young priest could see the four hands that moved irregularly and in exotic sequences about the great dial. His warning shout had barely echoed down to the square in front of the temple's entrance, where three of his fellows awaited the clock's coming in their robes of priesthood, before the space-time vehicle alighted and its passengers stepped forth.

They were immediately ushered into the temple, along a maze of corridors, until finally they came to that inner sanctum where Atal the Elder reclined upon his bed of silks. Extreme in age and fragile as he was, warm recognition still showed in the patriarch's faded, almost colorless eyes as he welcomed the two dreamers into his presence. His trembling, whispery voice was urgent as he gave them the grim news:

185

'My young friends . . . it is terrible . . . terrible!' he quavered. 'Sinister creatures in the city in greater numbers than ever before. Three of the temple's young priests bloodily slain – the lady Tiania of Elysia and the girl Litha Enderby of Ulthar kidnapped and carried off – and an almost tangible oppression settling like a shroud over the minds of all Ulthar's decent citizens. I set a dozen of my pigeons to seek you out – to Nir, Serannian, Hatheg, Sona-Nyl, and Baharna; even to Ilek-Vad, though I was not sure that the bird would be able to fly into the city – and I am only sorry that you . . . were not found . . . soon . . . enough . . .' He came to a faltering, panting halt.

'In your own time.' Titus Crow calmed him, quickly seating himself beside the centuried high priest, cradling his head and shoulders against his own strong arm. 'Now, from the beginning –'

And so, slowly and with many a pause, Atal told them how on the previous morning it had been noticed that there was an inordinate number of the strangely turbaned traders in the city, those squat beings of ill-legended Leng. Ulthar had never found it necessary to totally ban such creatures – only the trading of their blasphemous rubies was forbidden, and usually the horned ones were merely passing through the city on their way to less discerning places – but nevertheless Atal found this sudden increase in their numbers greatly disturbing.

He made discreet inquiries, discovered that furtive groups of the horned ones had been seen in that district where Tiania of Elysia was staying, and immediately his concern trebled – particularly when Grant Enderby himself later complained that he had seen suspicious evening shadows where none had been before, shadows that melted quickly away when he attempted to approach them.

Enderby had been sure that the horned ones were watching his house, and certainly his wide experience of these beings was such as must make him something of an expert on them. Thus he conveyed his concern for his exotic house guest to Atal, who in turn sent three priests from the Temple of the Elder Ones to watch over Enderby's house through the night. At the same time Atal gave orders that a dozen carrier pigeons were to be prepared for release to distant lands and cities, and with his own trembling hand he wrote the cryptograms to be tied to the legs of those blood-hued birds. All to no avail.

The straight, short ceremonial swords of the temple – with which the three young priests were not familiar in any other than esoteric connections – had been useless against the viciously curving blades of the horned ones, as the headless corpses of those priests had all too mutely testified the next morning. Enderby himself was lucky; he had been knocked unconscious from behind as he patrolled the walls around his house and garden. Mercifully his wife and sons had been away, visiting an ailing relative in a nearby hamlet.

At dawn, when the quarrier had achingly regained consciousness, he had found the decapitated priests lying in his garden where they had been dragged by their killers. Tiania of Elysia and Enderby's daughter Litha were nowhere to be found.

'And that,' Atal brought his tale to an end at last, 'was the way of it. Who can say what the rest of it will be?'

5

The Legions of Nightmare

As Atal finished speaking, Crow laid the patriarch's head gently back on the pillows and stood up. A wild rage shone in the dreamer's eyes and his whole attitude was that of a lion crouching before springing to the attack.

'De Marigny,' he grated, 'if ever I've felt sorry for my enemies before – if ever I've been guilty of feelings of sympathy for the CCD in their eternal banishment, or their dupes and minions caught up in the foul schemes of their prisoned masters – then may my soul *rot* before I ever shall again!'

And Henri-Laurent de Marigny, white and trembling with fury and horror, made his own vow. 'Atal, we leave the Temple of the Elder Ones now – and we shall not return until these great wrongs are righted and their authors punished in full . . .' He paused, then turned despairingly to Titus Crow. 'But where can we even begin to look for them – and for Litha and Tiania?'

Before Crow could answer, Atal spoke. 'Wait, wait! I have sent out birds, dozens of them, the temple's pigeons, to all towns and hamlets in the vicinity of Ulthar. If the horned ones have passed by any one of fifty places, we shall soon know of it. Indeed, some of the birds have already returned, but as yet they have brought no word. You will fly off in your time-clock, I suppose, but if you have no success before evening, call back this way. By then we may know something. The priest at the top of the tower . . . will be kept . . . fully informed . . .' And once more exhausted, he again lay back on his pillows.

Without another word, the two grim-faced dreamers

turned and left Atal's room, passing into the maze of corridors and making their way quickly out of the temple.

They split up, Crow taking the time-clock and de Marigny his anti-gravity cloak, flying outward from Ulthar in opposite directions to begin their aerial search of the surrounding regions. Crow headed for the coast, thinking that perhaps Kuranes had been right about a hidden sky-galley in which the horned ones would attempt an escape; and de Marigny followed the Skai down to distant Dylath-Leen, deserted now and strangely drab in the mid-afternoon sunlight.

Both dreamers were to find only bitter disappointment . . .

Titus Crow sought the sails of ships as he flew out over the sea – particularly ships headed for the horizon, where they might suddenly lift into the sky, bound perhaps for Kadath, Leng, or even dreamland's moon itself – and, sure enough, after searching for over an hour he spied sails, but these were already airborne. And they were not the ominous black galleys of the horned ones but the colorful battle-yachts of Serannian, on their way to Ulthar as Kuranes had promised.

Briefly Crow landed on the deck of the lead ship to inquire of the captain if perhaps anything had been seen of black galleys sailing the seas below. He was told that nothing had been seen at all to arouse any suspicion, neither on the Cerenarian nor on the Southern Sea. Crow quickly related what he knew of the recent trouble in Ulthar and took off again.

De Marigny, making ever widening, concentric sweeps about Dylath-Leen and eventually winging out over the great deserts, spied a caravan in an unseemly hurry and approached with some caution until he flew directly above it, unseen by its masters. But no, these were only honest merchants of dream about their business, and their haste was probably due to the close proximity of Dylath-Leen, whose gray towers reared in sinister fashion not too many miles distant. It would be a long time before that empty city lost its unenviable reputation in dreamland.

As the hours passed and afternoon began to grow toward evening, Titus Crow and Henri-Laurent de Marigny turned back for Ulthar. Over the City of Cats they spied one another across a league of sky, and winging down toward the tower of the temple both were attracted by the frantic waving of a priest behind the high, ivied parapet. They landed together on the roof, and as Crow stepped out of the time-clock de Marigny began to question the young, breathlessly excited priest.

Yes, at last there was news! A dozen of the horned ones, more furtive than ever, had been sighted in mid-morning on the outskirts of Nir. They had been making their way across the plain toward the Enchanted Wood, bearing two bundles like rolled carpets with open ends. And strange sounds had seemed to emanate from those bundles, like muffled cries for help. Later, a shepherd had found traces of the party in a cave, where they had doubtless rested out the night. Their journey must be very tiring; horned ones were not ideally structured for the carrying of heavy bundles, and they had no beasts of burden with them.

This news had come via one of the temple's carrier pigeons, sent back by a holy man in Nir, and it arrived just as Kuranes' sky-yachts had appeared over the city. With his vessel anchored firmly to the temple's high tower, the senior captain had alighted to learn of the kidnapping and of the route taken by the kidnappers toward the Enchanted Wood. The airborne ships had at once sailed off in the same direction, picking up a vengeful Grant Enderby and his sons on the way. This had occurred well over an hour ago.

'Into the clock, Henri!' Titus Crow cried. 'I believe I know what they're up to now, and if I'm right we haven't a moment to spare!'

'The Enchanted Wood, of course!' de Marigny exclaimed as the clock's door closed on them and they lifted to the sky. 'The Enchanted Wood – and that great slab with its massive ring and runic inscriptions!'

'Right,' Crow grimly affirmed, sending the clock racing across dreamland like a coffin-shaped blur in the sky. 'One of those places King Randolph Carter told us about – where Cthulhu's engines of nightmare pound away down in the black, reeking underworld, manufacturing madness with which to disease the subconscious minds of men and subvert them to his cause. It's a place like the one we destroyed beyond the Peaks of Throk, whose guardian was the vast and leprous Keeper. I only hope we're in time, that's all.'

Far down below, the grassy fields of the plain rushed by breathtakingly; then, ahead and to the left, Nir appeared, drew level, vanished behind in a twinkling; the singing Skai flashed for an instant like a narrow silver ribbon in the last rays of evening; Hatheg with its domed dwellings came and went. In the twilight they overtook the battle-yachts of Serannian and at last flew over the edge of the gloomy Enchanted Wood.

Then Crow reluctantly reduced the speed of their craft and brought it down to the level of the treetops in the rapidly fading light, and as the rush of the great trees beneath them slowed they covered another mile or so until they came to that shocking region of diseased oaks which was in fact almost a clearing of crumbling stumps, quaggy earth, and luminescent, bloated fungi. There Crow set the clock down and they alighted from its cleanly pulsating radiance into the rotten glow of putrefying foliage.

They carefully approached the center of that scabrous clearing, where lay the massive slab with its Titan ring. Eagerly their eyes searched the mold and mush-slimed edges of the great slab for signs that it had recently been moved.

'Thank all that's merciful!' cried de Marigny, his voice shattering the miasmal silence. 'It hasn't been moved. We're in time, Titus!'

Crow nodded in the semidarkness. 'Yes, if this is indeed their destination –' He suddenly cocked his head on one side and held up a cautionary finger. 'Listen! Do you hear it? What do you make of that, Henri?'

All was gloom, fetor, and uneasy, misted silence. De Marigny held his breath and listened for a moment. He could hear nothing. 'What is it, Titus?'

'Here, put your hand on the slab. Now do you hear it?'

'Yes . . . It's a pounding, deep down in the bowels of the earth.'

'Well, we were right about that at least.' Crow nodded in grim satisfaction. 'This is certainly the portal to one of Cthulhu's factories of nightmare. And –'

'*Shh!*' de Marigny suddenly whispered. 'Someone's coming!'

A moment later came definite sounds of disturbed underbrush not too far distant – immediately followed by an outraged cry from a female throat!

'Litha!' de Marigny choked, instinctively making to rush in the direction of the cry.

'Hold on, Henri,' Crow restrained him. 'Believe me I'm as eager to be at them as you are, but let's get the time-clock out of the way first and lie in wait for them. Let's see if we can discover just exactly what's going on here.'

No sooner had they flown the time-clock into a deep, dense patch of bramble at the edge of the clearing, closing its panel behind them so that the clock's weird light would not give away their presence, than from the opposite side of the clearing appeared the fugitive group of horned ones.

Between them – hands bound and shivering, with their clothes in tatters – staggered the two fiercely protesting girls, Tiania and Litha. Crow and de Marigny saw all of this very clearly, for two of the horned ones had lanterns that cast a yellow, penetrating light all about as they moved forward, dragging the women toward the great slab.

'Titus,' whispered de Marigny, his hand trembling violently on the other's arm, 'I can't –'

'*Shh!*' Crow cut him off. 'The girls are all right, Henri, just a bit roughed up, that's all. Let's learn what we can before we make a move.'

In the center of the clearing one of the horned ones moved forward, held up his lantern before him, and commenced to read from the runes graven into the top of the slab. Such sounds as he made could never be echoed by the vocal chords of man, but the horned one was totally fluent in this unearthly tongue. And in response to the chanted rune, suddenly, with a harsh grating and shuddering, the great slab began to tilt upon some hidden spindle. As the horned one continued his weird chanting, so the girls were bundled forward.

'All right, Henri,' Crow snapped, urgently gripping his friend's shoulder. 'Now see what you can do to slow things down a bit while I bring the time-clock into play!'

De Marigny needed no more urging. He bounded aloft in his cloak, swooped down from on high, and crashed headlong into three of the squat creatures from Leng. One of these flew with a shrill shriek straight into the reeking gap where the edge of the slab had now lifted to reveal an inky hole beneath; a second was dashed to the mushy earth where he lay still; the third jumped to his feet – only to be grabbed about his fat neck and hoisted aloft as de Marigny flew his cloak up into darkness. A moment later and this third horned one's gurgling cry was cut off short as his squat body fell with a snapping of bones against the steadily tilting slab.

A few seconds more and de Marigny flashed out of the sky again – but this time they were ready for him. Four of them were still awkwardly struggling with the girls, doing their best to push them into the hole showing beneath the slab while keeping a nervous watch out for de Marigny. The other five slashed with their scimitars at the dreamer's hurtling form as he swerved over their heads.

Then Titus Crow took a hand in the matter. The time-clock crashed forward out of the brambles at the clearing's edge; and even as the horned ones saw that strange vehicle of the Elder Gods, so Crow triggered the clock's awesome weapon.

A beam of purest, dazzling light flashed forth from the four-handed dial, slicing first into those five horned ones whose blades were drawn against de Marigny, scything them down in an instant. The four who held the girls let go of them at once and turned to flee. Crow cut three down with another slashing beam of light, then, with that same beam, tracked the fourth – who immediately darted behind the now almost vertical slab!

Crow's beam struck the great slab . . . and the next instant the whole clearing shook with an ear-splitting roar as that monstrous door to the underworld shattered and flew asunder. It was sheer luck that the two girls, stumbling away toward the edge of the clearing, were not hit by the boulder-sized chunks of rock that hurtled in all directions; but they were not, and when the smoke cleared they stood clinging together, half-swooning, until de Marigny alighted beside them and hugged them to him.

Only then, when it appeared that the immediate danger was past, did the true horror of the situation become apparent.

For as de Marigny stood with his arms protectively about the two girls – and as Crow in the time-clock surveyed the scene in the clearing, ill-lit now that the lanterns of the horned ones were extinguished – so there came a subterranean rumbling and a geyser of slime and foul gases from the yawning pit. Hurriedly, half-carrying the girls with him, de Marigny backed away from that awful orifice; but Titus Crow, protected by the almost totally impervious shell of the time-clock, eased his vessel forward until it poised on the very lip of the pit.

Using the clock's scanners he gazed down into a dim and reeking abyss . . . *from which, suddenly and without warning, there burst a noisome stream of horrors straight out of a madman's blackest nightmares!*

Ethereal the things might well have been, but still they seemed solid enough to cause Crow to back his clock hastily away from the pit's edge. Dozens, hundreds of them, out they poured like pus from a ruptured abscess, an endless tide of monsters created by Cthulhu's machineries of madness, released now to plague the subconscious minds of mortal dreamers. And they were, quite literally – *nightmares!*

Misty, wraithlike, utterly malignant and malevolent, they swirled and billowed about the poisoned clearing while their shapes seemed to take on more form, more substance. Here were vampires, ghouls, werewolves and witches, monsters of every sort imaginable and others quite unimaginable. Burnt-out eye-sockets leered from melting faces; mad fangs gnashed hideously in mouths that drooled and chomped vacuously; eyestalks twined and twisted while leprous claws and stumps of fingers scrabbled spastically. The stenches of a thousand open tombs issued up from that hellish pit, and its gibbering depths reverberated with a throbbing cacophony of completely lunatic, utterly inhuman laughter.

And the worst was still to come, for de Marigny and the girls had no protection at all against these nightmares from the pit, which now swarmed about them in ever thickening, ever more threatening hordes. Illumined in the rotten glow of phosphorescent corruption, Crow saw the faces of the three convulse in ultimate horror, watched them quite literally going mad in the face of unthinkable, unbearable nightmare.

Again and again, frantically he triggered the clock's weapon, lighting up the clearing in blinding flashes of white light, shredding the monsters from the pit in their hundreds. But as quickly as they steamed off in vile evaporation others rushed from the hole to replace them. Then the unimaginable happened: suddenly Titus Crow himself was on the defensive!

At last he recognized his peril and cursed himself that he hadn't seen it sooner. These things were *nightmares*, and even in the dreamlands they were not 'physical' but 'psychical' phenomena. As such they were not subject to mundane laws of time and space. He could no more keep them out of the time-clock than he could keep from dreaming. Dreams come and go ignoring all walls and barriers – and so do nightmares!

Again he triggered the clock's mighty weapon, again, and yet again . . . until at last he felt his brain gripped and wrenched and squeezed by incredible terror, and knew that finally they had breached the time-clock's polydimensional walls! Then everything seemed to dissolve in one vast cataclysmic bombburst of flame and light . . .

6

Nyarlathotep

For a single moment only – which Titus Crow reasonably believed might be his last – the blinding glare filled the clearing with its light, leaving a cascade of illusory fireworks dripping white fire on his retinae . . . and leaving his mind completely free from nightmare!

Instinctively, in complete astonishment, he had time enough to merely glance into the clock's scanners before turning from them to avoid suffering the glare again. For in the night sky above the Enchanted Wood he had seen a glad, fantastic sight: six battle-yachts in line, their ray-projectors aimed threateningly down into the heart of the nightmare-ridden clearing. The clearing itself had looked much as before, except that now the mist was that much denser through absorbing the ectoplasmic stuff of which a thousand defunct nightmares had recently been composed.

De Marigny, Tiania, and Litha had been stumbling to and fro, their hands to their heads, still suffering the mental aftermath of that concerted attack of blackest nightmares; and even as Crow had snapped shut his scanners to avoid the blaze of a second salvo from the ray-projectors, he had seen that the gaping, steaming pit still issued a vile stream of threatening, abyss-spawned horrors.

Flying blind but using all the skill with which his long experience of the time-clock had endowed him, he flew across the clearing, skirting the pit to fetch a halt close to the stricken trio. As he made to leave his exotic, hybrid machine – even within its hyperdimensional shell – still

Crow felt again that blast of awesome illumination as the aerial gunners opened up on the nightmares from the pit a second time; then he quickly stepped out of the clock, snatched up Tiania, and pulled her to safety. He did the same for Litha and finally de Marigny, and no sooner was the clock's door shut than yet again there came a concerted blast of purifying light from the sky.

Only then did Titus Crow use the scanners again, and as he lifted the clock up out of the clearing he saw that the rush of nightmares from the subterranean abyss was greatly reduced. A few seconds later he landed his vessel beneath the mainmast of the lead ship and assisted his rapidly recovering passengers out onto the deck.

'Titus,' de Marigny caught his elbow as he turned back to the clock. 'What are you doing?'

'I intend to finish this job once and for all, Henri. Don't worry, I'm not going down into the pit. I just intend to close it up forever – if I can! These shipboard ray-projectors are fine used en masse, and their powers must be very similar to the clock's own, but I think you'll find they're only good for short bursts. This job will require more than that.'

Without another word he entered the clock and flew it back down to the clearing, hovering directly above the pit. Only a thin trickle of nightmares was issuing from that ghastly hole now, and keen-sighted gunners on the battle-yachts were picking them off as fast as they appeared. Crow tilted the clock slightly, lining up its four-handed dial with the mouth of the pit, then triggered his weapon in a long, continuous burst.

And Titus Crow was right, for while in unison the ray-projectors were indeed a force to be reckoned with, as individual weapons they simply could not be compared with the marvelous power of the Elder Gods. Directly into the mouth of the pit he played that unbearably pure beam, illuminating incredible depths that seemed to go down forever, perhaps to the vaults at dreamland's core. For thirty seconds or more that stream of concentrated purity – the very Essence of Benevolence, the evil-destroying Light of the Elder Gods themselves – played into the pit, and slowly but surely the desired metamorphosis was brought about.

First the mushy ground in the immediate vicinity of the pit began to glow with a radiance of its own, a light that throbbed like the beating of a great luminous heart. And this radiance spread outwards until it encompassed the entire clearing, pulsing ever faster, almost hypnotically, in a strange strobic splendor.

At the height of this activity – from which at its onset, as from a suddenly erupting volcano, the six sky-yachts had sailed off to a safe distance – without warning the ground in the clearing began to bubble and boil, flowing like molten lava and streaming into the pit. On the heels of this phenomenon came others as the entire clearing and the diseased oaks around it suddenly trembled, then heaved and bucked in a seismic convulsion as muffled explosions sounded from deep down in the underworld. Then, blowing outward from the spot where the pit had been, there came a howling, madly rushing ghost-wind that hurled the six sky-yachts back across the sky like so many autumn leaves, a torrent of winds that continued long after Crow released the trigger of his awesome weapon. The ground in the clearing still steamed and bubbled, and it retained a little of its luminosity – in which eerie light Crow now witnessed the beginning of this strange drama's final act.

Slowly at first, then rapidly widening, a crack appeared in the glowing earth where the pit had been sealed off, and emerging from this ominous fissure came a rotten, greenish glow that seemed to ooze upward into the clearing. At first Crow was tempted to use the time-clock's weapon yet again, without waiting to see what this new threat might be, but his human curiosity got the better of him. Despite his recent experience with the nightmares from the pit, his faith in the clock's imperviousness remained all but unshaken; whatever this green glow was he did not believe it could harm him. In any case, it would be the work of the merest moment to bring his weapon to bear upon this unknown thing, for its 'trigger' was in his own mind. He flew the time-clock down to a spot which he reckoned was at a safe distance from the as yet unidentified phenomenon.

The glowing sphere of green light slowly lost its opaque quality until Crow could make out a figure standing at its center – a human figure! And as the green glow grew dimmer yet and the winds ceased their frantic outward rush, so he made out the physical details of this unexpected apparition.

Tall and slim, clad in bright robes and crowned with a luminous yellow pshent, the figure seemed to become more solid as its heralding green glow died away. It was a man with the young, proud face of a Pharaoh of ancient Khem – but whose eyes were those of a dark God, where lurked a languid, sardonic humor.

'So you are the man Titus Crow,' the figure finally spoke in rippling mellow tones. 'A mere man – and yet much *more* than a man . . .'

On hearing that languorous voice – despite detecting a trace of malice in the emphasized word, which ought to have alerted, galvanized him – a creeping numbness fell over Crow's brain. Too late, he started to reach out a mental finger, intending to activate the time-clock's weapon, only to discover that halfway to the trigger his hand was stayed, his will frozen solid. An iciness like the chill of the deeps between the stars pervaded his whole being, robbing him of all volition. And at last Titus Crow recognized the newcomer, knew also that he was face to face with Doom, that he could not possibly survive the encounter. For this handsome young Pharaoh was none other than Nyarlathotep, the Crawling Chaos!

'Ah, yes!' The voice came inside Crow's head now. 'You know me, Titus Crow, for we've had dealings before, you and I, when you've seen me in some of my thousand other forms. And you are one who knows me for what I really am, and you know the nature of my masters . . .

'Well, dreamer, it is at an end. Only a very few men have caused my masters so much concern, and doubtless you would go on to cause more trouble if you were not curbed. For you are impetuous and wild and do not understand my masters, who are great and glorious beyond all greatness and glory. So I have sought you out in dreams, and have brought about this meeting which will set your feet on the road to a greater destiny: to be one with my masters out among the stars and in the hidden places of the waking world!

'For they would like to know you, Titus Crow, more intimately. They would like to watch your reactions to terrors greater than any yet conceived by your race, and would taste of the entire range of your passions when, at the end, they scatter the shreds of your subconscious being to the very corners of existence. But never fear, Titus Crow, for they would not destroy you immediately. No, for there are punishments far worse than those imposed upon my masters by the so-called Elder Gods, and surely a suitable one will be found for you . . .

'Now come, dreamer, out of your time-clock and embrace me. Come, for we have far to go and must leave at once . . .' And Nyarlathotep beckoned, smiling sardonically and opening his arms wide as if welcoming an old friend.

Like a doll on the strings of a master puppeteer, Crow opened the clock and stepped out of its purple-glowing interior. He approached Nyarlathotep wide-eyed, moving like an automaton, and as the distance closed between them so the green glow began to return, springing up and deepening around the slim Pharaoh-like figure.

Behind the dreamer as he moved inexorably forward, the weird purple light from the open door of the time-clock grew deeper as its pulsing slowed; the glow itself expanded until it completely encompassed the clock and a wide area around it, finally matching in size and intensity the green and rotten luminescence about the form of Nyarlathotep. Abruptly in Crow's frozen mind a second commanding voice now resounded:

'Man of Earth, you, Titus Crow, *stop!* Turn about!'

Falteringly, zombie-like in his movements, the dreamer turned. A vast nebulous face was growing out of the purple glow about the clock, a face in which huge golden octopus eyes glared out in a terrible rage. Face-tentacles lashed and the entire visage of the Elder God shook and trembled in the spasms of a towering passion.

For this was of course the image of Kthanid, Tiania's guardian and Titus Crow's patron in Elysia – Kthanid, who now used the time-clock more truly as a gateway between dimensions to intrude on Crow's behalf in this his moment of direst peril.

'Titus Crow, come to me!' ordered Nyarlathotep, his mental voice slightly less mellow, less certain now. Obediently, the dreamer began to turn away from the clock.

'No!' came Kthanid's urgent denial. 'Get out of the way if you can, Titus, so that I may strike him. I have a power here greater even than the time-clock's own. But it will destroy you, too, if you stand before it!'

'He can't disobey me, fool!' Nyarlathotep laughed, his voice quickly deteriorating to a bass croaking in Crow's mind. 'Come to me, Earthman – NOW!'

At that precise moment, down from the sky a bat-cloaked figure flew, hurling the stumbling, hypnotized dreamer from between the two beings in the clearing. Immediately the spell was broken; Crow shuddered as he clung to de Marigny and they lifted up above the treetops of the Enchanted Wood. Then, rising rapidly toward the sky-yachts, the two dreamers stared down at a fantastic scene.

A tremendous booming voice came up to them, a mental voice that reverberated in their minds as Kthanid addressed his Enemy: 'You have threatened those in my protection – even Tiania who is flesh of my flesh – *and now you must pay!*'

Simultaneous with the last word, twin beams of pulsating golden light flashed from Kthanid's great eyes to penetrate the green glow of corruption and strike the figure of Nyarlathotep with their full force. He staggered, that Great Messenger of the CCD, then swelled up huge and bloated. 'Damn you, Kthanid! Let me . . . *go!*'

'Not until you have suffered . . . and would that I could make you suffer a thousand times more!' Again the twin beams leapt from his eyes to the grotesquely bloated figure of the Pharaoh – which instantly reformed itself into . . . *something else!*

A vast, monstrous congeries of iridescent globes and bubbles shifted and frothed where the bloated human figure had stood, and Kthanid's cry was glad and triumphant as he hurled his beams directly into this seething mass. Those sizzling golden beams struck home – and for a moment the two dreamers floating high above were afforded a glimpse of the *Thing* that lurked behind those globes and bubbles: a Titan primal jelly of wriggling ropes, bulging eyes, and tossing, convulsing pseudopods and mouths – an ultraevil, supersentient anemone from deepest oceans of horror!

'Ah, Yog-Sothoth! So, you have helped Him in this, have you? A joint effort, was it? And who else hides behind the lying mask of Nyarlathotep, how many more of the thousand forms?' Again the searing golden beams lashed out, and another metamorphosis immediately took

place. Gone now the liquescent, purplish-blue loathsomeness of Yog-Sothoth, and in his place a towering black
anthropomorphic outline that stood on great webbed feet
and gazed with carmine stars for eyes!

'Ithaqua, too!' boomed Kthanid. 'The Thing that Walks
on the Wind. Well, begone, Ithaqua, and let us see what
others there are . . .'

Then, in rapid succession, using his twin golden beams
like great knives, Kthanid peeled away the outer layers
of telepathic consciousness that shielded the innermost,
ultimate blasphemy. Many members of the CCD there
were that Crow and de Marigny recognized, and many
they did not know at all. Shudde-M'ell was there, the
dreaded burrower beneath; yes, and fiery Cthugha and
tentacled Hastur, too. A single, shocking glimpse of
slimy Yibb-Tstll; and one of Yig, Father of Serpents; and
Zhar, Chaugnar Faugn, and many others. And finally –
Cthulhu!

Cthulhu, the dread Lord of R'lyeh, dreaming but not
dead, sending his dreams from drowned R'lyeh to infest
and desecrate the sacred lands of Earth's human dreamers. He was almost the twin of Kthanid, but where Kthanid
was golden Cthulhu was leaden, where the former was
Good the latter was absolute Evil. Evil writhed and
twisted in twining face-tentacles, leered out of kraken
eyes, and twitched convulsively in vastly arched wings.
Evil glowered hideously, unblinkingly at the shining image
of Kthanid – until once again, for the last time, twin beams
of pulsating yellow fire reached out to strike the monster
dead center.

'Get you gone from here, Cthulhu,' boomed the Elder
God, 'back to R'lyeh where you belong. Will you never
learn to keep your mad dreams to yourself? Begone!'

Then there echoed up from the clearing a tremendous,
rumbling explosion like a great clap of thunder, and when
the dazed dreamers flying high above next dared to look

down Cthulhu was indeed gone. Gone, too, was Kthanid, and the time-clock stood alone and issued its softly pulsing glow in a clearing that lay blasted and barren and silent, where, in the morning, birds might safely sing as they never had since time immemorial . . .

Epilogue

Ah, yes, the Inn of a Thousand Sleeping Cats, in Ulthar! Of course, I didn't hear all of the tale that one evening, merely snatches of it that reached me from the fabled group at the head of the massive banquet table. The Enderbys were there – with dark-eyed Litha seated blushingly alongside Henri-Laurent de Marigny – and Tiania of Elysia, side by side with her Earthman, Titus Crow; and all around the table were dignitaries from all of dreamland's districts and counties and cities. Yes, even Atal of Hatheg-Kla. And all of them come to applaud the exploits of the adventurers from the waking world.

As to the tale's total veracity: well, I for one would swear to it. Have I not myself visited the Enchanted Wood and chatted with the Zoogs, all of them telling me of that night when the wood was bright with strange lights, following which the birds returned to nest in the great oaks about the place where once had rested a monstrous slab of stone graven with strange runes?

Aye, and there are other proofs. I have already booked passage on a galley out of Theelys bound for Dylath-Leen, and who would once have braved that place? And what captain dared to sail his ship there? Too, bright sky-yachts float above dreamland's cities and patrol her farthest borders, reporting their findings back to ever-watchful Kuranes in Serannian and King Carter in Ilek-Vad. And I'm told that so far they've had precious little to report, for which I'm glad.

But it must not be believed that the Forces of Evil are finished in dreamland. No, for beyond the frontiers of sanity there still lie lands of ill-legend and temples of terror. Leng breeds her horrors as of old on the borders of dream, and Kadath broods gray and gaunt in the Cold Waste. Aye, and man is an infant in dreams compared with great Cthulhu, who slumbers on eternally in R'lyeh, waiting . . . waiting.

And what of the heroes of the story now? Well, I have it on good authority that de Marigny is dreaming a white-walled villa in timeless Celephais, to which he'll return one day when at last he's traveled the road to Elysia. And Tiania and Titus Crow?

Strange visions wake. Fearsome starlanes and the gulfs between dimensions beckon. How long before even the marvels and wonders of dreamland pall and the lure of the Unknown calls Crow and his love away again? Who can say?

Worlds without end.